DESTINY

Caroline Flack

contents

CHAPTER 1

It's been 4 months, 2 weeks and 23 minutes since I last talked to him. I tried not to think about it but it was kind of hard to do so when he was everywhere. Not literally but I saw him everywhere I looked, on my phone, at school, in movies, he's just everywhere.

My friends didn't know I was still thinking about him, I told them it was over and that I was done talking to him. But, he still haunts my dreams in the day and in the night.

I miss him so much and not talking to him hurts but talking to him hurts even more.

I got up out of bed and dragged myself to the bathroom to brush my teeth. I looked in the mirror and my hair was a mess as usual, I didn't really care these days though, I didn't have any energy so I just decided to leave it.

I did my business and went into the kitchen to have some breakfast. I fried some eggs and bacon and ate it with some bread and a cup of ginger tea. My breakfast wasn't very fulfilling but whatever, it would have to do.

I was finishing up cleaning when I heard my phone ring. Annoyed, my first thought was to ignore it. I was in no mood to have a conversation with anyone at the moment but I looked at the phone anyway.

"Hmm", I thought.

Why was Ashley calling me? I swear the girl cannot go a day without feeling the need to tell me about her business but then again I kind of enjoy it.

I picked up the phone and braced myself for the immediate chatter. I wasn't proven wrong when I barely finished saying hello before she cut me off.

"You will not believe what happened today? Enrico asked me out, I was just making a coffee run when I stumbled into him and we were talking about that new movie that came out and he was like do you want to go watch it together and I totally freaked out and screamed yes.

This Saturday, I can't believe it."

"That's great Ash, I'm really happy for you". Ashley has been crushing on this guy since she started working at Forest enterprise and finally got her wish. As I praised her for finally getting her wish I couldn't help but feel a pang of hurt.

She must have noticed the change in my tone because she asked"hey babe are you okay?"

"I'll be okay, everything happens for a reason I guess", that's what I've been telling myself for the past 20 years of my life. You see, my family has labeled me as 'cursed'. Whenever I'm around, shit always seems to hit the fan. As for my life, well you can say it's a mess.

I sighed for the 100th time today. "I'm fine"

"Did you find any jobs yet?"

"Nope"

I was seconds away from bursting into tears. What did I ever do to deserve such cruelty?. I lost my job and the love of my life in the span of two months. Yeah I was far from fine.

My life has been a wreck ever since I was a child. My parents knew this and tried to avoid me at all costs. By avoiding me I mean sending me to borading school for practically all my life and when I got a chance to go home they would send me to stay with my aunt.

I realized they treated me differently since I was 8. It was my birthday that day and despite the fact that everyone was behaving weird I woke and ran downstairs expecting my parents to be down there welcoming me with open arms,spoiling me with gifts but instead I was greeted with an empty house and a cold plate of an egg sandwich lying on the kitchen counter.

I was eight, you would think they would atleast left someone with me at home but no, they left an underage girl child all alone at home on her birthday.

Luckily, I matured a lot faster than most kids, so with my shoulders sunked I grabbed the sandwich, got a chair and stood on it so I could reach the microwave to heat it up then grabbed a bottle of orange juice from the fridge and had my breakfast.

I went and sat down on the couch when I noticed a sticky note lying on the center table. I picked it up and looked at it with disappointment.

Happy birthday hunny, sorry we couldnt be there when you woke up, had some errands to run. Lock the doors and eat whatevers in the house we won't be back until tonight.

End of note.

I was eight.

From that moment on, I realized that it was just me, myself and I. I left as soon as I turned eighteen and moved in with my boyfriend the one that dumped me.

He had links and hooked me up with a job at a call center near his apartment. I was getting a good pay and I had a loving boyfriend what could go wrong?

Except everything did.

I found out he was involved in some human trafficking business and was planning on selling me too but I found out before it was too late and got put under police protective services.

I didn't have any siblings, at least that's what I'm aware of but, my parents refused to take me in. They said they didn't have the time or space to look after me.

They live in a 2 story house.

Luckily by that time I had saved up enough money to rent a small apartment and buy some food to live.

My friend Ashley wanted me to stay with her but she lives with her friend and I didn't want to intrude but, from time to time she buys me groceries which I really appreciate because the little money I have left is running out quickly.

"Liv, are you still there", I snapped put of my thoughts as I heard Ashley calling me.

"Hey I have to go now but I'm coming over later", she said.

I nodded even though she couldn't see me "sure", I answered and hang up the phone.

At first I refused her help but I couldn't anymore, if I did I would starve to death. All the money I have left is for the landlord after that I don't know what I'll do.

The money is supposed to last for the next two weeks after that I'm positive he's going to throw me out if I don't pay him.

I sighed again for who knows how many times today. This is fantasic. I finished eating my breakfast and then continued searching through the news paper for a job.

So what do you guys think?Remember to leave comments and a vote.

CHAPTER 2

It was now evening and I was starving, I looked in my purse and saw a dollar. Great, I thought.

I put on a coat and grabbed my phone before heading outside. As I closed the door I saw that the handle looked like it was about to break off.

"Are you kidding me", I screamed in frustration, kicking the door making the handle actually falling off.

"Hey are you okay?", a voice suddenly called out.

I jumped suddenly startled by the voice but looked to see a guy looking at me curiously.

He was standing at a door, two doors down from mine. I looked at him for a second then spun around and went downstairs and went outside totally ignoring him.

I'll admit it was a bit rude but I was hungry and when I was hungry I didn't give a shit so it sucked to be him.

I got out of the apartment building and started walking down the street when I saw a little girl and her mother dancing. They were in their yard dancing away not having a care in the world. That seemed so nice, I'm glad the child was going to grow up and have an actual childhood.

I looked away before I started thinking about my mom. Over the years I've figured out how to not feel sad about them but from time to time I can't help but wonder why they hated me. I get that I was basically bad luck but I was still their child.

I was still in thought when I bumped into someone. "Ouch!", the person exclaimed. I looked up and saw that it was a girl. She looked a bit older than me

and she was really tall like 6ft but then again I was 5ft 5 so everyone above 5 ft 7 was tall in my eyes.

"Hey I'm sorry, I wasn't looking where I was going", I said quietly.

She then smiled the biggest smile I have ever seen in my life "oh no worries hun, I wasn't looking where I was going either. I got a text and I took it out of my bag to look at it when I bumped into you so I guess it's both our fault."

I just smiled in return "My name is Olivia but my friend calls me Liv", I said holding my hands out to her to which she quickly shook my hands in return. "I'm Sofia and my friends call me, well Sofia", she said laughing.

"Okay Sofia", I said laughing too.

"Are you from here?"

"Umm, yeah, yeah I am", I answered feeling a bit uncomfortable.

Either she didn't notice or she didn't care but she kept smiling as she asked me for my number. I paused debating if I should or not. Every friend I have ever had was fake and didn't stay very long but I decided to give it a shot. What's the worst that could happen?

So I gave in and we exchanged numbers. She told me she lived nearby and that we should catch up sometimes. I just answered with a sure. I was probably not going to be here for long anyways.

After we parted our ways I remembered why I was walking in the first place. Oh yes, I was starving.

That Sofia girl seemed nice but I doubt she would stay, they never do. I walked a bit further before I came to the dollar store.

I went inside and bought a cheap chocolate bar and went outside to eat it. Looking at the time I saw that it was 5 Pm. Ashley should be coming now so I headed back home.

I was climbing up the staircase when I heard someone talking on their phone. They were in front of me so I couldn't see their faces.

"I know that, you think I don't know that, every day I think about it so you don't need to keep rubbing it in my face everytime you call. I've got it okay"

I didn't want to eavesdrop so I fastened my pace and tried to pass them. My efforts were left futile when I felt someone grabbed my arm. " What the heck is wrong with you?", I shouted as we both came to a stop at the top of the staircase."Don't touch me".

"Okay,okay I'm sorry, it's just that I wanted to ask why you ignored me earlier"

I didn't even realize that it was the guy I saw before. I mentally rolled my eyes at my horrible luck.

"What are you talking about", I inquired.

"You know well what I'm talking about", he said, coming closer to me, causing me to step back against the wall. " I was asking if you were okay and you just ignored me without answering" , he said as his gaze softened.

I looked at him blankly, I can't believe this guy, who was he to act as if he knew me. "Look man I didn't hear you okay now can you back up?".

He nodded and then backed away from me, I was about to walk off when he grabbed my hand again. I quickly pulled away, "Listen asshole if you touch me again you won't keep that arm of yours.

"Hey, hey I'm sorry I just wanted to know your name"

"No", I said walking off.

"No", I heard him shout behind me.

"My name is Sebastian by the way"

"Don't care Stanly", I shouted back.

I didn't turn around but I heard him chuckling, I only rolled my eyes in return.I walked up to my door and went in to see Ashley laying on my couch.

"Hey Ash", I called to her. She looked at me happily." Hey babe where were you?".

I shrugged " went for a walk"

She came up to me and gave me a hug " I brought pizza", she whispered in my ear causing me to smile. What would I do without her?.

Remember to vote and let me know what you think.

What do you think about Olivia, do you think the guy was being rude?

CHAPTER 3

"Okay so I'm thinking that I should wear a dress but I don't know if I should, it's probably too much for the movies right?"

"Yeah true but what if he plans to take you home after", I answered teasingly.

Ashley gasped in embarrassment, if her skin tone was light her cheeks would be a bright red right now. But her dark skin prevented such.

I always envied how flawless her skin was, the girl never had a pimple and her skin always looked cool like she just washed it. Whereas my dark brown skin felt like it was drenched in oil and acne was basically my best friend. We were both black but it was obvious who had the better features here.

"Hey you never know, I mean you are gorgeous, from your skin to your hazel eyes to your body. He would be a fool to not take you home."

"You know I'm not like that, I need a man who will treasure my purity. If he only wants sex what's the point? But I don't think he's like that. We have been friends for some time now and you could say I know him"

I rolled my eyes while taking up another slice of pizza. "Yeah that's what they all say until they seduce you into their bed then end up leaving you, men are trash Ash", I chuckled at my ryhming.

Ashley grabbed the pizza from my hand and took a huge bite "Not all men are trash you know you just haven't met the right one yet"

"Whatever helps you sleep better at night babe"

"You are so annoying", Ash answered, rolling her eyes.

"Yeah but you still love me", I said, sticking my tongue out at her.

"I'm just gonna stick with a tank top and jeans with a jacket"

"Sounds good enough but make sure you bring a condom too"

"Olivia!"

"Haha, just kidding"

I got up and went into the mini kitchen and saw that Ashley already packed away the groceries she bought me. How long had she been here before I came?.

I pushed away the thought as I got a bottle of water and went back into the living room where I saw Ash scrolling through her phone.

She looked up when she heard me coming and quickly put away her phone. "What's up?", I asked suspiciously.

"It's nothing, anyway I have some good news, Forest enterprise is Hiring"

"Wait really?"

"Yeah, they're looking for a receptionist. This is your chance".

I sat down beside her, getting this job would really help me out I would finally be able to pay rent and have money for food. "Okay I'm in how do I apply?"

"I could drop off your resume for you"

"Yes, thank you, thank you", I said excitedly kissing her on the cheek.

I ran into my room and quickly grabbed Ashley's old laptap that she gave me and quickly edited my resume then ran down the road to an internet Cafe to print it and gave it to her.

She looked at it and nodded "I'll put in a good word for you and fingers crossed they'll call you back for an interview. "

"Thanks Ash I really don't know what I would do without you, you gave me food, money and clothes sometimes when you didn't have to. Which I am going to give back and before you protest don't.

I'm going to buy you something with my first check okay so don't even try to convince me otherwise. You were there when I had no one, I love you from the bottom of my heart Ash, I really do", I said getting emotional.

" Don't you dare cry or else I'm going to start crying and you know when I cry it's not pretty.", she said sniffing.

" You literally cannot be ugly no matter what you do", I cried.

"I love you too, okay okay I have to get home now"

I released her and wiped my eyes as I watched her leave. She really was my everything. I was feeling kind of icky so I decided to take a shower then went to bed, praying that I got a call back for an interview.

I think we should all have a friend that has our back no matter what, don't you agree?

Remember to comment and drop a vote see ya next time

Chapter 4

A week had passed and I had yet to receive a call about an interview, I sighed at my horrible luck. Why did I think that this would work out for me? I'm going to be homeless soon and I was going to starve to death not long after.

Luckily I still had groceries that Ash bought, I got out of bed and made breakfast. I wanted to go out today and see if I could get a job at Walmart or any supermarket. I already looked and they didn't have any job vacancies available but I would beg if I had to because I was desperate.

I slowly chewed my food trying to savor every bite so it keeps me full. I was already skinny and I was afraid of losing more weight but I don't exactly have a choice in the food I get to eat.

I took a shower and got out of my apartment. I hissed my teeth in annoyance when I saw the state of the handle. The landlord made it clear that he would not pay for any damages done to his property made by me but when I came here it was falling off already. I tried explaining to him that I didn't do this but he didn't listen.

Now anyone can come in if they try. I sighed in defeat, slowly twisting the handle in an attempt to keep it on its hinges.

Suddenly, I heard a noise so I quickly snapped my neck in the direction but saw nothing. Hmm, odd I thought. I didn't really pay it any mind as I headed outside.

I walked and walked until I reached a supermarket called flying dragon. I went inside and saw that it was busy, everyone was running around trying to help customers and the lines to the cashier were really long.

I saw a guy pushing a cart around the store so I walked towards him. His back was facing me so I cleared my throat and gently touched his shoulder. "Ahh, oh shit what!"he screamed, turning around.

Stepping back and putting my hands up in defense I said "Hey man sorry, how are you so easily frightened?"

"Haha, I'm not, I was just in deep thought you know", he said, scratching his neck nervously.

I raised my eyebrows not believing him "right.....anyways I was wondering who I could talk to about getting a job here"

"Ah yes you can talk to the manager I can bring you to her if you want"

"Yes that would be amazing thank you"

"Alrighty little lady follow me"

"I'm not little", I muttered following him.

"Yeahhh you are", he answered laughing, clearly hearing what I said.

"My name is Alex by the way"

"Hi Alex I'm Liv"

"Okay here we are", he said, showing me a door that had the sign 'manager' written on it.

"Thank you so much Alex", I said, turning around to look at him.

"No problem Liv", he answered winking then walked off.

I turned around facing the door taking a deep breath as I raised my hand to knock.

"Come in ", I heard a voice answer. I gulped as I opened the door and went in, she sounded harsh I thought.

"How can I help you?"

"Hi, my name is Olivia and I was wondering if I could get a job here, literally anything would be great.", I said.

She looked me up and down then looked back down on her desk at some papers. "We don't have any vacancies for full time at the moment but, there is a space for part time if you're interested".

"Yes, yes I'll take it", I almost shouted getting excited. It wasn't full time so I wouldn't be getting as much money but it's still something.

"Okay Olivia can you come in on Saturday at 2Pm for an interview?"

"Yes I can"

"Alright"

"Thank you for the opportunity miss..."

"Garvey"

"Thank you again miss Garvey, I'll see you Saturday", I said waiting for her to dismis me but she just looked back down at her papers so I took that as my cue to leave.

I walked out and was about to leave when I heard Alex calling me, I turned around smiling at him "Hey how was it?"

"Coming in for an interview Saturday"

"Nice"

"Its only part time though but it will have to do"

"Well guess we'll get to see each other more often little lady"

I glared at him and walked off "I'm not little!".

I walked back to the apartment but immediately stopped when I saw my door. The handle was fixed, did the landlord have a sudden change of heart?.

I looked around and went to my neighbour and knocked on her door to ask if she saw something but she didn't answer. I huffed in annoyance because I knew she was in there because I literally hear her inside talking.

I spun around and decided to just confront George the landlord. I reached his office and knocked until I heard him tell me to come in.

"Hey George, I just want to say thanks for fixing my door handle. I'm glad you finally believed that I didn't do it, I'm relieved because anyone could have broke in if they tried so thanks.", I said smiling.

George only looked up at me with a bored expression. "I didn't change it, your neighbour did"

I looked at him confused, "Why would hailey fix my lock the girl doesn't like anyone"

"Who's Hailey?"

"My neighbour", I said getting irritated.

"Oh yeah yeah no, I meant your other neighbour the one that recently came in, the tall light brown dude, think his name is Sab, Sebtain, something like that"

"Sebastian??", I asked shocked. Why did he fix it?, gosh I cannot take anymore shit in my life right now especially from a guy.

"Yes that's the one, he came to me and I opened the door so he could fix it, don't worry I watched him the entire time he didn't go through your things or anything creepy like that he just fixed it and left.

He's quite handsome are you two together?, you know I looked a lot like him back in my day", George said laughing.

"I highly doubt that", I answered scrunching up my face.

He immediately scowled at me "well if there isn't anything else...", he trailed off.

"Yeah yeah, bye", I said taking my leave.

I can't believe he fixed my handle, he didn't even know me. It was obvious he was desperate for attention and I wasn't going to give it to him. I went back to my room and went inside looking at my apartment to ensure everything was still in place and went to prepare something to eat.

Hmm, what do you think guys?, Why did you think he fixed her lock?

Remember to vote and drop a comment or two.

Until next time

CHAPTER 5

The incessant buzz of my phone jarred me awake, and I hastily reached to silence the relentless device. I rubbed my eyes, half-asleep, and answered the call without checking the caller ID.

"Hello, my name is Janet Howard from Forest Enterprise. Is this Olivia Hunter?"

I scrambled to sit up properly, attempting to collect my thoughts. "Yes, this is her."

"Excellent. We've carefully reviewed your resume and believe you might be a suitable fit for the receptionist position. Could you make it for an interview this Friday at 2 PM?"

"Yes, absolutely," I replied, striving to sound composed.

"Great. Please remember to bring your birth certificate, ID, qualifications, and so forth."

"Thank you, Janet, for this opportunity."

"You're welcome. Have a nice day."

"You too."

As soon as I ended the call, I couldn't contain my excitement. It was almost unbelievable – a potential job on the horizon. Not just one interview, but two.

I leaped out of bed with joy and quickly dialed Ashley's number. I couldn't wait to express my gratitude.

The phone rang and rang until I heard, "You have reached the voice-mail box of..."

I hung up, unperturbed. She was at work so it made sense that she didn't pick up but she always calls after leaving work so I'll just wait until then.

The realization hit me like a ton of bricks that Friday was the day after tomorrow. I quickly ran to my suitcase where I had a few clothes and pulled them all out and realized that I had absolutely nothing to wear.

Nothing suitable for an interview that is. Sighing I made a note to ask Ashley for a skirt and maybe I could pair it with one of these shirts I have.

In the evening, I prepared my necessary documents, placing them in an envelope and then in my bag. I cooked a meal of fried chicken and white rice and washed it down with a bottle of water, and cleaned up. Then I sat on the couch, scrolling through social media.

I wasn't really active on social media like that. He was the social butterfly out of the two of us. I logged into instagram and saw that I had a few dms. They were just a few guys trying to ask me out.

I rolled my eyes and logged off. The last thing I needed was another relationship. I'd learned that nothing seemed to go right for me in that department.

My thoughts drifted to Sebastian. He was undeniably attractive and appeared to be a good guy. But my heartbreak was still fresh, and I wasn't ready to move on.

I browsed through my phone's gallery,which usually contained mostly pictures of him and I but I deleted them, leaving a few selfies and some with Ashley.

Feeling bored, I turned on the TV, but there was nothing interesting going on. Just as my frustration began to set in, my phone rang.

Excitedly, I answered, "Thank goodness you called, Ash. I was about to die from boredom."

"Haha, I saw you called earlier, but I was busy."

"I understand. I wanted to share some news – I've been called back for an interview."

"Really? That's fantastic! When is it?"

"It's this Friday, and I need to borrow some clothes. Can you help me out?"

"Of course, you don't even need to ask. I won't make it over tonight, but I'll drop by tomorrow evening."

I sighed in relief. "Thanks, Ash. Text me when you get home so I know you're safe."

"Sure, bye and congratulations."

"Goodbye."

I ended the call and found myself bored once more. So, I decided to watch some humorous videos on YouTube until I drifted off to sleep.

<><><><><><><><>Thursday evening quickly arrived, and with it, a sense of anticipation. I couldn't wait for Ashley to come over and bring the clothes for me to borrow and help me prepare for the interview.

The doorbell rang, and I rushed to answer it. Ashley greeted me with a warm smile and a big hug. "Congratulations on getting the interview, Liv!"

"Thanks, Ash! I don't know what I'd do without you," I replied, genuinely grateful for her support.

With a bag in her hand, Ashley said, "I brought the clothes we discussed for you to borrow."

We went to my bedroom, and Ashley pulled out the smart black skirt and crisp white blouse she'd selected. "These will make a great impression. You'll look professional and confident."

I nodded in agreement. "Perfect choice, Ash. Thank you."

Ashley then turned her attention to my hairstyle. "How are you going to do your hair for the interview?"

I contemplated for a moment. "I think a neat bun would work."

"Okay so I have some products here you can use to help slick back your hair. I also have my hairdryer here cause we know how stubborn your hair is so I'm gonna help you blow it out now then tomorrow morning you can comb it.

I snickered at what she said, but it is true though everyone knows black hair is no joke.

As we moved on to makeup, she gave me a few things to keep it light and natural, accentuating my best features without overdoing it. "You want to look like yourself, just a more polished version," she advised.

I couldn't help but smile. Ashley was not just a friend but a true life-saver. She helped me gain the confidence I needed for the interview.

Once we were done with the outfit and grooming, Ashley reassured me, "You've got this, Liv. You're smart, capable, and you've got a fantastic friend here who believes in you."

I hugged her tightly. "Thank you, Ash. I don't know what I'd do without you. You've made such a difference."

We spent the rest of the evening practicing interview questions and talking about the job and what it could mean for my future. Ashley's encouragement and support gave me the boost I needed.

As the evening wore on, she finally said, "You're going to do great, Liv. Now, get a good night's sleep, and I'll be here tomorrow before your big day."

I nodded, overwhelmed with gratitude for the friend who had been there for me when I needed it most. Ashley's presence was a reassuring comfort, and I couldn't wait for the opportunity that lay ahead of me.

With Ashley's help, I felt ready to face the interview and whatever challenges life had in store for me.

Remember to vote

CHAPTER 6

The morning sun streamed through my curtains, and I woke up with a sense of determination. It was the day of the interview, and I felt surprisingly calm, thanks to Ashley's support the previous evening.

I got out of bed, dressed in the professional outfit she had brought for me. The black skirt and white blouse fit perfectly, and I felt a renewed sense of confidence as I looked in the mirror.

Ashley arrived as promised, carrying a thermos of coffee and a few breakfast snacks. "To kickstart your big day!" she said with a smile.

I thanked her and we sat down, sharing a light breakfast together. As we chatted, Ashley encouraged me to stay positive and remember my strengths. She reminded me of all the hard work and determination I had put into this moment.

With our meal finished, we began a final review of some common interview questions and answers. Ashley acted as the interviewer, asking questions and providing constructive feedback on my responses. This practice helped me fine-tune my responses and boosted my confidence.

The good thing about where I'm going is that Ashley works there too so I got my bag, ensuring I had everything necessary and we headed to the interview location together.

In the waiting room, I took a few deep breaths to calm my nerves. Ashley gave me an encouraging pat on the back and waited with me until it was time to go in.

Finally, it was my turn. I walked into the interview room, greeted by a panel of interviewers, including Janet Howard. I felt ready, polished, and confident, just as Ashley had helped me become.

The interview went smoothly, and I answered questions with assurance. When it concluded, I walked out with a sense of accomplishment, knowing I had given it my best.

Ashley was waiting outside, her supportive smile welcoming me back. "You did it, Liv! I'm so proud of you!"

I couldn't help but feel grateful for Ashley's unwavering support. Her presence and encouragement had made all the difference in this crucial moment of my life.

As I walked back home, I couldn't be certain of the outcome, but one thing was for sure - I had faced the interview with confidence and determination, thanks to Ashley's friendship and support.

When I reached home, I got something to eat, had a shower and basically scrolled through Social Media for the rest of the day. I know my life was really sad but hopefully I got the job and then I'll be able to go out and have an actual life.

Speaking of jobs, I forgot I had another interview tomorrow at that supermarket. All my documents were already in my bag so I just ironed another skirt and blouse Ashley left with me to prepare for tomorrow.

I smiled to myself knowingly, all I needed to have was just a bit of patience and everything would work out. I was in a good mood so I put some music on and danced around the house then put on a movie to watch. After which I went to bed ready to face the next day.

<><><><><><><><><><>The next morning rolled in and I did my business as usual and prepared for the interview. At exactly 2pm I was at the supermarket heading towards the manager's office. I was looking for Alex but I didn't see him so I just went where I was going.

I knocked until I heard her telling me to come in. "Ms. Olivia, please have a seat, how are you today?". She said smiling.

She looked weird and suspicious smiling because she looked like someone that would eat me for breakfast the last time I was here so the fact that she looked so cheerful seemed odd but maybe it's finally my lucky day so I played along.

"I'm great, Ms Garvey I'm alive and well so I can't complain you know"

She only nodded and looked at me then cleared her throat and began speaking. "So there has been a recent change in events taking place here at Flying Dragon, you see the supermarket has been sold."

"What!"

"Please calm down Ms Olivia", she said looking annoyed.

"As I was saying, the supermarket has been sold and the new owner has their employees already so the position you are applying for has unfortunately been filled. I do apologize for the inconvenience but this was a sudden decision and it is out of my hands."

I was shocked beyond words. "Um-uh, what about the other workers here will they be fired?", I asked my mind, suddenly going to Alex.

Ms. Garvey raised her brows at me "Some of them will be fired, yes, is there anything else?".

"No"

"Okay have a good day and again I'm truly sorry, I wish you all the best on your journey to come."

I only nodded as I left her office, all hope wasn't lost I thought. I still had another job I could get into. I looked around trying to find Alex but couldn't find him.

I stopped a worker asking where Alex was but they only told me he wasn't here today.I really hope they didn't fire him, I thought as I went home.

Thanks for reading, remember to press that vote button and drop a comment or two.

Didn't really like these two Chapters but they were necessary. Anyways until next time

CHAPTER 7

I was sitting on my couch watching a movie when my phone rang, I saw that it was Sofia calling me. I picked it up smiling. "Hey Sofia"

"Heyy Liv, how are you?"

"I'm good, what's up?"

"I was just here thinking that we should meet up, are you free later?".

"Uhh, yeah I'm free, what do you have in mind?"

"You wanna meet up at happy's bar? it's not far from where I saw you"

"Yeah I know the place but I'm broke"

"Don't worry it's on me"

Nodding, I said "What time exactly?"

"How about in an hour?"

"Sure no problem see you then"

"Cool".

I couldn't help but smile as I ended the call with Sofia. It had been a while since I went out to just have a drink and have fun. I was so busy stressing out trying to find a job and I probably had gray hairs growing in places they shouldn't be, I grimaced at the thought.

I quickly turned off the movie on my TV and got up from the couch, to get ready for our meetup at Happy's bar.

As I rummaged through my suitcase with limited clothes I tried to find something suitable to wear, my mind raced with excitement as I picked out a casual yet stylish outfit, not wanting to overdress but also not underdoing it. A quick shower, some light makeup, and a touch of my favorite perfume had me feeling ready for the evening.

With time to spare, I decided to tidy up my living room, making sure my apartment was in order. I glanced at myself in the mirror one last time, a sense of anticipation building as I imagined the fun evening ahead.

An hour later, I was out the door, heading to Happy's bar with a spring in my step, totally forgetting about the interview I had earlier. The call from Sofia had brightened my day, and I was looking forward to a night of laughter, catching up, and perhaps a few drinks, all thanks to my thoughtful friend that I now had.

I arrived at Happy's bar, and as I walked in I spotted Sofia sitting at a cozy corner table, a welcoming smile on her face. The atmosphere in the bar was lively, with the chatter of patrons and the soft murmur of music in the background.

Sofia waved at me to come over, "Hey," Sofia greeted with a warm hug. "I'm so glad you could make it."

I returned the hug, feeling the warmth of our new friendship. "Thanks for inviting me, Sofia. I really needed this."

"No problem".

We spent the evening chatting, sharing stories, and getting to know each other. Sofia was amazing and it felt like I knew her all my life. The drinks flowed, and laughter filled the air and I was thankful for this gathering, a much-needed escape from the routine of my life. I really needed to just get away and take a breath to calm down.

As the night went on, Sofia reached for the check, insisting on covering it as she had promised earlier. I smiled sadly as I remembered the situation I was in but a part of me still had hope, I just needed Forest enterprise to come through for me.

Sofia looked at me and softened her gaze at me as she placed her hand on mine. "Hey are you okay?", she asked.

She looked at me with the softest gaze I've ever seen. I only just noticed how beautiful she actually was. Her green eyes looked like the darkest parts of a cold Forest under the light and her pale skin shone beautifully. Her plump lips pursed together softly as she said something. What was she saying? It was like she was talking but no words were coming out, it was then that I realized how blurry everyone had become.

"Olivia!"Sofia calling snapped me out of my weird day dream. Shaking my head trying to get rid of the buzzing I tried getting up to leave but Sofia stopped me. "Hey, I think someone had a little bit too much to drink. How about you sit down for a bit longer, hmm?"

I followed her command as I sat back down and took a bottle she then handed me. "Now what were you saying?"

I stared at her confused then I remembered "oh yeah I was just kind of down right now because you know I'm broke and I don't have a job and my landlord is probably going to kick me out when I don't give him his money next week. "

"Oh my Olivia, can't your parents help you out?, you didn't mention them earlier"

I glared at her "look Sofia this was great but I think I should go now"

Sofia suddenly looked confused "Did I say something wrong? if I did I'm truly sorry"

"It's nothing, I'm just messed up, it's not you trust me. The good thing though is that I did an interview at Forest enterprise so hopefully I get it", I said yawning.

"Ohh Forest enterprise, I know that company. They specialize in various aspects of environmental and natural resource management. They are involved in activities such as sustainable forestry, wildlife conservation, and land management. Right?"

"Yep that's right"

"Anyways, I think that's enough for tonight . Text you later?"

" Yeah, that sounds great"

I left the bar, feeling a bit tipsy but better. I had totally enjoyed my night and was ready to curl up in my bed and sleep.

I was about to head inside when I saw Sebastian smoking outside. He didn't seem to see me yet so I decided to startle him "polluting the environment are you now?, didn't take you for a smoker.

Totally unfazed he just laughed "well now you know". He didn't turn to me as he blew out a puff of smoke. "You want?"he asked, finally turning in my direction.

Staring at his outstretched hand I wondered if I should even continue this conversation but after a second I gave in and took the cigarette from him. We sat down at his door in silence as we savored the moment.

"Why did you fix my lock?"I asked the question that was itching my mind.

He didn't say anything for a while as he stared into space "I wanted to apologize for the other day, I crossed your boundaries and I'm sorry."

I turned to look at him, but he didn't turn to look at me. There was something different about him I could see it , it's like something happened. He almost looked kind of sad but I decided not to ask and just nodded.

"I'm not going to say it was okay because it wasn't but I accept your apology and thank you for fixing my handle. "

He didn't answer as he took the cigarette and placed it between his lips.

"So Sebastian huh?"I said, trying to break the awkward silence.

Smiling he answered "yeah", as he finally turned around to look at me.

CHAPTER 8

It was now 10 Pm and Sebastian and I were still sitting at his door talking about the most random stuff.

Apparently he owned 5 cats and 5 dogs. To say I was shocked was an understatement. He definitely does not look like the type of person to have so many animals.

"You should have seen his face when he realized that one of my dogs shit on his shoes", Sebastian said, barely breathing as he laughed hard.

I couldn't help but burst into laughter while clutching my stomach, hoping it would alleviate the cramps.

"No way, so what did you do?", I asked in between laughs.

Sebastian gasped as he tried to catch his breath and wiped away a tear that was now rolling down his cheek. "I took one look at the shoe and one look at him grabbed Lex and ran for the hills"

I gasped as I hit him "you didn't"

He looked at me smirking "oh yes I did, to be fair he deserved it after he nearly ran over Lex then refused to apologize saying it wasn't his fault when it was clearly his fault.

He was an asshole and I don't regret a thing. I just went home and gave Lex a big treat for being such a smart dog"

We looked at each other for a second or two before we burst out laughing again

"I bet he had a great day"

"I bet"

I was about to say something when I heard a door burst open behind me " if you too love birds are done laughing I would like to get some sleep, yall aren't the only ones in this building you know", Hailey our neighbor said looking annoyed in her sponge bob pajamas.

"Nice pjs hailey", Sebastian said smirking.

"Ughh talk to your man before my fist does it for you", Hailey said looking at me. But before I could say that he wasn't my man she went back in and slammed the door.

"What is her problem?"

I looked at him knowingly, "You're a troublemaker, you know that?"

He only shrugged coming closer to me "oh really"

"Yes", I said as my heart started beating faster. The closer he came the faster it started beating. "W-a What-t are you doing?"

He came closer until he was directly right in front of me and I could feel the heat of his breath on my face. "What does it look like I'm doing?"

"I-", I was about to speak when my phone started ringing, I gulped as I quickly answered the call. "Hello this is John King calling from Forest Enterprise, is this Olivia Hunter?"

Confused I looked down at the phone then put it back at my ear "Yes this is she"

"Okay good, I hope I didn't bother you by calling you at this time but our customer service team works twenty four seven and we were instructed to make the call as soon as possible.

We had an emergency meeting today to finalize our decision, and it took longer than anticipated. We also encountered some technical issues with our communication system, which delayed our notifications to candidates."

"No, no, it's not a problem at all, I was just umm watching TV", I said as I looked at Sebastian who was now staring at me curiously.

"Good to hear, right so we know you had an interview the other day and we want to express our sincere gratitude for your interest in our company and the time you invested in the recent interview.

It's evident that you have impressive qualifications and experience, which made our decision particularly challenging.

After careful consideration, we've chosen another candidate for the position. While your qualifications were highly regarded, we had to make a difficult choice based on the specific requirements of the role.

We want to emphasize that this decision is not a reflection of your abilities or potential, but rather a result of our specific needs at this time.

We understand how disappointing this news can be, and we genuinely appreciate your understanding. If you'd like, we can provide more specific feedback about the decision and areas where you excelled during the interview.

We hope that you find a rewarding opportunity that aligns with your career goals, and we wish you all the best in your job sear-."

My ears started ringing as the phone slipped out of my hand and my eyes started filling with tears as I tried to make sense of what I just heard. I didn't get the job. Why does this always happen to me, why me?, why?.

I didn't even realize that Sebastian took the phone and hung up the call. "Olivia what happened, are you okay?"he asked, looking at me like he was worried.

"No, no, leave me alone", I muttered.

"What's wrong, come on tell me", he said trying to hold my hand but I pulled away from him.

"No you need to get it through your thick skull that I don't like you, we are not a thing.

I don't even know you, so stop trying to get with me because it's never gonna happen okay. Are you that desperate for female attention?. You're pathetic, just leave me alone.", I shouted as I got up and took my phone, ran to my door, quickly opened it, went inside and started breaking down, not sparing Sebastian a glance."

I could hear Sebastian knocking on the door, telling me to open up but I refused to listen. I fell in my bed and cried and cried until I fell asleep, hoping that this was all a dream.

Remember to vote an comment.

CHAPTER 9

I remained in bed for the better part of the day, the heavy weight of disappointment holding me down.

I didn't want to face the world or the reality of my situation. It wasn't until evening that I mustered the strength to sit up and glance at my phone, which lay abandoned on the bedside table.

Ashley had left several missed calls and messages. She had been trying to reach me throughout the day, and I felt a pang of guilt for not responding. My friend was always there for me, and I should have let her know what I was going through.

Just as I was contemplating returning Ashley's call, there was a knock on my door. Ashley's voice called out from the other side, filled with both concern and determination, "Liv, it's me. Open up."

I quickly wiped away the remaining traces of tears from my eyes and made my way to the door. Ashley walked in, her expression a mix of relief and worry.

"Liv, I've been trying to get in touch with you all day," she said, her voice tinged with concern. "I didn't get any response from your phone, and I was really worried. What's going on?"

I finally confessed, "Ashley, I didn't get the job. They called last night, and I was devastated. I haven't been able to bring myself to do anything all day."

Ashley wrapped her arms around me in a comforting hug. "I'm so sorry to hear that, Liv. But we're going to get through this together," she reassured me. "You're not alone in this."

As the evening turned into night, Ashley made it her mission to lift my spirits. She knew I was facing not only disappointment but also the daunting prospect of unpaid bills. With determination, she convinced me to step out of my apartment, even if just for a little while, to clear my mind.

We took a walk through the city, and Ashley shared stories of her own past setbacks and how she had overcome them. She assured me that we'd find a way to tackle the financial hurdles together, emphasizing that friends support each other through both good and bad times.

The weight on my chest didn't disappear entirely, but with Ashley's unwavering friendship, it became a little easier to bear. We faced the uncertain road ahead together, knowing that even in my darkest moments, I had someone by my side who cared deeply about my well-being. But even then I was still sad.

"It's the curse Ash, it won't leave me alone"

"Stop that nonsense, you're not cursed, you're just going through a rough time in your life right now. You'll soon see the light, trust me."

"Yeah I'll see the light alright, when I'm dead"

"Olivia!"

"What?, you say I'm just going through a rough time in my life right now, well guess what I've been going through it since I came out of the womb and I don't know how much more of this I can take. "

Ashley immediately stopped walking which caused me to stop too. "Look at me, I'm here and I'm not going anywhere I know it might be hard right now but I'm right here, you hear me?"

Nodding I took a deep breath listening to the birds chirping and the gentle wisper of the wind, I felt it softly touch my skin and comb through hair as if trying to soothe me "Okay"

"Yeah?"

"Yeah"

We were sitting on a bench in the square park when I saw someone waving and coming in our direction.

"Do you know her?", Ashley asked.

Squinting my eyes to get a better look at the person as they came closer I realized that it was Sofia.

"Yeah that's Sofia"

"Who's Sofia?"

"A girl I met some time ago, we actually hang out last night"

Ashley looked back at Sofia who had now reached the bench we were now sitting at "Hey Liv, I was taking a walk when I saw you"

Looking up at her I smiled and turned towards Ashley "Ashley this is Sofia, Sofia this is my sister from another mother Ashley."

"Hi, Ashley it's nice to meet you"

"Likewise"

"Can I join you guys?"

I looked at Ash and she nodded "Yeah, yeah, have a seat"

Sitting down beside me Sofia looked at me and said "Why do you look like that is something wrong?"

"How do I look?"

"Sad"

"Oh", I said looking down.

"I didn't get the job", I said trying not to cry. Ash must of noticed because she started rubbing my arm soothingly.

"What!, I can't believe those assholes. I'm so sorry to hear that Liv I'm sure you deserved it. "

Nodding I started playing with my fingers.

"What are you going to do now?"

"I don't know"

Sofia didn't answer as she was lost in thought.

"How about we go out and try to forget everything for now?"

Before I could answer Ashley spoke for me "I don't think that's a good idea, she just wants to chill right now.

Nodding I looked at Sofia "Yeah I agree I just want to relax and try to figure out what I'm going to do.

"Come onnn", she whined. "You need this, trust me you'll feel better. Alcohol makes everything better I promise.

"I highly doubt that"

"Please come on, everything is on me I promise.

I looked at Ashley silently asking her what she thinks. "Okay, Liv if you want to, I'm up for it."

Looking back at Sofia I sighed "Fine, but we're not doing anything crazy".

Sofia suddenly grinned "No promises", she said winking.

Why do I feel like I would regret this?

Remember to vote and comment

CHAPTER 10

As we sat in the park discussing our impromptu plan to go out with Sofia, I couldn't help but feel a mix of trepidation and curiosity.

From what I could tell Sofia had an adventurous spirit, and I knew that a night out with her could be unpredictable.

Nevertheless, I decided to embrace the idea, if only to momentarily escape the heavy cloud of disappointment that had been hanging over me.

"Okay, we're doing this," I said with a determined nod. "But Sofia remember no crazy antics, alright?"

Sofia grinned mischievously. "I promise, Liv. Just a little fun to lift your spirits."

Ashley chimed in, "Don't worry Liv I will be here if anything happens."

With our plan set, we returned to my apartment briefly to freshen up. I changed into something more suitable for a night out, and we made our way to a nearby bar that Sofia had recommended.

The bar was lively, with the chatter of patrons and the music creating an inviting atmosphere.

We found a cozy corner to settle in, and Sofia immediately took charge, ordering a round of drinks for all of us. As the evening progressed, we laughed, shared stories, and enjoyed the live music that filled the air.

It was refreshing to have this change of scenery and a break from my worries. For a while, the weight on my chest seemed to lighten, and I genuinely smiled. I was reminded of the simple joys of being in the company of friends.

The music throbbed, and the laughter was infectious. The cares and disappointments that had weighed me down earlier in the day began to fade into the background.

For a moment, I felt free and light, as if the curse I had mentioned earlier was losing its grip.

The club was a vibrant and energetic place, filled with a diverse crowd of people looking to let loose and have a good time.

The dimly lit room was bathed in a variety of colorful neon lights that pulsed in time with the music. The bass thumped through the floor, creating a palpable energy that seemed to seep into every corner of the space.

A mix of music genres flowed from the DJ's booth, from pulsating electronic beats to catchy pop tunes and even some classic rock hits.

The dance floor was packed with revelers moving to the rhythm of the music, their bodies swaying and grooving with an infectious enthusiasm.

Couples twirled and spun, groups of friends formed impromptu dance circles, and strangers found themselves dancing side by side. Laughter and conversations blended with the music, creating a joyful cacophony that filled the air.

The bar was a bustling hub of activity, with bartenders expertly mixing cocktails and pouring shots.

The clinking of glasses and the occasional cheer from those taking a shot added to the lively atmosphere. The scent of various drinks, from fruity cocktails to aged whiskey, wafted through the air, creating a heady aroma.

There were moments of sheer abandon, as people let go of their inhibitions, their laughter ringing out above the music. Some danced with wild abandon, while others showcased their best dance moves with flair and confidence.

It was a place where you could be yourself, free from judgment, and simply enjoy the moment.

As the night wore on, Sofia convinced me to hit the dance floor. I wasn't much of a dancer, but with a little encouragement and some liquid courage,

I found myself letting loose and dancing like no one was watching. Ashley joined in and we formed our little circle of celebration, forgetting our troubles for a while.

The music enveloped us, and the lights danced upon our faces. We moved with the rhythm, losing ourselves in the joy of the moment, our cares and worries momentarily forgotten.

It was a night filled with laughter, music, and camaraderie, a stark contrast to the heavy disappointment that had marked the day.

As the hours passed, the club remained alive with energy, a sanctuary where people could come together to celebrate life and friendship, and for a little while, escape the burdens of the world outside.

Amid the vibrant and energetic atmosphere of the club, my eyes scanned the crowd, and then I saw him. Sebastian, he stood near the bar in a more relaxed and casual attire.

He wore a well-fitted black T-shirt that accentuated his toned physique, paired with a pair of dark jeans that exuded a stylish yet laid-back vibe.

His rugged, tousled hair fell casually across his forehead, giving him an effortlessly attractive look.

The dim, colorful lights of the club still highlighted his sharp features, but this time, he seemed more approachable and at ease.

Seeing Sebastian in this more relaxed state ignited a different set of emotions within me. My previous encounter with him had been filled with tension.

I felt a sudden rush of embarrassment and regret for my previous behavior. The memory of that encounter when I had cursed him off out of frustration and embarrassment made me cringe.

It was as if my past actions were magnified under the club's vibrant lights.

The weight of disappointment that I had momentarily forgotten seemed to return and it now mingled with an uncomfortable feeling of self-consciousness.

I hesitated, unsure of whether to approach Sebastian and make amends or to simply continue dancing and ignore the situation. I couldn't help but wonder

what he thought of me after what happened . The thought of facing him under these circumstances was both nerve-wracking and intriguing, adding an unexpected layer of complexity to my night out.

As the music continued to pulse around me, I contemplated my next move, after a while I decided to go up to him.

I slowly walked through the crowd of heated bodies until I reached where he was standing surrounded by two guys and a few girls.

As I approached I saw the look of shock on his face. "Hi Sebastian", I said nervously.

"Hey"

His friends were now staring at me and I felt their eyes putting me under a microscope. "Ugh can we talk?"

Cleaning his throat he nodded "Hey see you later", he said to his friends then turned to me "How about we get out of here"

Nodding, I told him that I was going to tell my friends first. Scanning the crowd I spotted Ashley and Sofia chatting away. "Hey guys I think I'm gonna head out now"

Ashley looked at me worriedly "Are you alright?"

"Yeah I'm just a bit tired right now"

"Do you need me to come?"

"No, no just go home, we will talk tomorrow."

"Olivia, are you sure?"

"Yes mom", I said, rolling my eyes.

"Liv I'm serious"

"I'm sorry Ash, yes I'm okay."

"Okay I'm going to head out now too then I'll drove you home".

"Ugh", I said scratching my neck.

"My neighbor is bringing me home".

"Your neighbor, Hailey?".

"No, umm, Sebastian he recently came in".

"How come I don't know him?".

"He's new Ash".

Sighing she gave in "Fine but text me when you get home".

"Okay good night and thank you for just being here, you're amazing. We'll talk tomorrow".

Turning to Sofia and hugging her I said " tonight has been great thank you".

"No problem Liv, I hope everything works out for you and if you need me just hit me up."

Smiling, I said "bye guys.

Going back to Sebastian I told him I was ready and he just nodded and we left the bar and went to his car.

Remember to vote and comment

Chapter 11

As we left the vibrant atmosphere of the club and stepped out into the cool night air, the contrast was striking. The thumping bass and colorful lights were replaced by the quiet darkness of the street.

I was acutely aware of the change in dynamics, from the loud and lively club to the intimacy of the car.

Sebastian opened the door for me, and I slid into the passenger seat. He started the engine, and we drove off, the city's lights illuminating the night around us. There was a comfortable silence in the car as we navigated through the city.

As the city lights faded in the rearview mirror, I couldn't help but feel a mix of emotions. The night had taken unexpected turns, from a carefree night out with friends to a chance encounter with Sebastian, the source of my earlier embarrassment.

Now, we were on our way somewhere unknown, and my curiosity warred with my lingering doubts.

I couldn't help but steal glances at Sebastian from the corner of my eye. His profile was softly illuminated by the dashboard lights, and I found myself drawn to his features.

The tension from our previous encounter seemed to have dissipated, replaced by an unspoken understanding of the night's events.

After a while, he spoke, breaking the silence. "I didn't expect to see you here tonight, Liv."

I nodded, feeling a bit self-conscious. "Yeah, it was a last-minute decision. Needed a break from everything."

"I see".

"I owe you an apology," I said, looking at him earnestly.

"It was not your fault and I had no right to say those things to you, it's just that nothing ever seems to go right for me, and you were there and we were talking and for a second everything felt like it was okay.

For a second I felt normal, and then just like that my bubble was burst and the realization that it wasn't real came crashing in and I just snapped and you didn't deserve that I'm sorry."

He smiled, and it was a warm, forgiving smile. "No need to apologize. We all have our moments, and I'm not holding it against you."

"I mean I'm not going go to pretend to know what you're going through but I just want to be here for you as a friend or anything more", he said glancing at me and winking.

Laughing I said "Not even in your dreams".

We continued driving in a comfortable silence for a while, the city lights gradually giving way to a quieter, more suburban area. The night air flowed through the open car windows, carrying the scent of blooming flowers and fresh grass.

After some time, I finally asked, "Sebastian, where are we going?"

He glanced at me with a mischievous smile. "It's a surprise, Liv. I promise it's something to take your mind off things and have a little fun."

I couldn't help but feel a mixture of excitement and apprehension. "Okay, I trust you."

"Really?"

"Of course not"

"Haha, you wound me love"

Sebastian continued driving until we reached a secluded beach, the sound of the ocean waves gently breaking against the shore filling the air. He parked the car, and we stepped out, the cool night breeze caressing our skin.

The beach was bathed in moonlight, casting a silver glow over the sand. The sound of the waves and the distant lights of the city created a tranquil and almost surreal atmosphere.

Sebastian extended his hand to me. "Care for a walk on the beach?"

I took his hand, and we strolled along the shoreline, the gentle waves washing over our feet. The weight of my earlier disappointments and the chaos of the club seemed to fade away in the serenity of the night.

The gentle ebb and flow of the waves served as a soothing backdrop to our conversation as Sebastian and I continued to walk along the moonlit beach. We shared our dreams, our fears, and our experiences, finding common ground and discovering the layers of each other's lives.

Sebastian talked about his love for photography and his desire to capture the world's beauty through his lens. He described his travels, the diverse people he had met, and the profound moments he had witnessed. Listening to his words, I found myself drawn to his passion and the genuine enthusiasm he had for life.

In turn, I shared my aspirations, my love for literature, and my desire to find a job that would allow me to make a meaningful impact. The disappointments I had faced in my job search didn't define me; they were just temporary setbacks on the path to something greater. Sebastian listened attentively, offering words of encouragement and understanding.

As we walked along the shore, I couldn't help but feel that the beach held a certain magic. The waves whispered secrets of hope and possibility, and the moon painted a canvas of dreams in the night sky. In that moment, I realized that life was a journey, and sometimes, unexpected detours could lead to the most beautiful destinations.

We sat down on the sand, our feet gently submerged in the cool water. The stars above us sparkled like diamonds, and the night seemed endless.

Sebastian's presence was a comforting anchor, and I felt a newfound sense of serenity.

"You know, Liv," he began, his voice soft and contemplative, "life can be full of surprises. It can throw challenges at us that we never expected, and sometimes, it can feel like we're lost in the darkness. But it's during those times that we discover our inner strength and resilience."

I looked down in thought for a moment "Pain is all I've ever known, from my parents, from my friends, from guys, it's a constant cycle of pain. You say I'm discovering my strength but what if I don't want to be strong.

I was a child, I didn't need to be strong I needed to be loved and cared for. I'm just so tired."

He put his fingers beneath my chin and raised it so I was now looking at him "Hey, you didn't deserve what happened to you, but it happened. You survived and because of that you're now a strong and beautiful woman."

I looked at him, captivated by his words and lost is his eyes "You're right. I've faced setbacks, but I can't let them define me. I want to keep moving forward, even if it means taking a different path."

Sebastian nodded, his eyes reflecting the moon's gentle glow. "That's the spirit, Liv. Life isn't about avoiding obstacles; it's about finding a way through them. And sometimes, the most unexpected people and moments can guide us."

Under the moonlight, I couldn't help but see Sebastian in a different light. The tension and misunderstandings that had marked our first encounters had given way to a genuine connection. As we continued to talk and share our stories, I realized that the night had become a turning point, a moment when two people from different worlds found common ground.

Sebastian suddenly looked up and pointed to the sky. "Look, a shooting star."

I followed his gaze and spotted the streak of light, a fleeting moment of magic in the night sky.

Sebastian turned to me, his eyes filled with sincerity. "Make a wish, Liv."

I closed my eyes and made a wish, the words a silent plea for a brighter future. When I opened my eyes, I met Sebastian's gaze, and for the first time, I saw a connection that went beyond the surface.

The night was almost over, and as we walked back to his car, I couldn't help but feel that this unexpected journey was leading me to a place of hope and possibilities. The heavy cloud of disappointment had begun to lift, and I started to believe that better days were ahead.

He drove us home and we went inside stopping at my apartment door. "Thank you for tonight, I really appreciate it"

Smiling he ruffled my hair "No problem Olivia"

"Hey!"

"Hi", he answered laughing.

"Remember, life is full of surprises, and sometimes, they can be the most beautiful moments. If you ever need someone to talk to or simply a friend to share your journey with, you know where to find me."

Nodding, we exchanged numbers promising to stay in touch. Then we said our goodbyes.

As I entered my apartment, I couldn't help but reflect on the unexpected turn of events. The night had started with trepidation and uncertainty, but it had evolved into a memorable and transformative experience.

The weight on my chest had lifted, replaced by the hope that, just like the shooting star we had witnessed, my wishes might just come true in the end.

CHAPTER 12

The days that followed brought with them a renewed sense of purpose. Sebastian's words and the time we had spent together on the beach had a profound impact on me. I was determined to overcome the disappointments in my job search and take a fresh approach.

I dove back into my job search, revising my resume and reaching out to various contacts. The setbacks no longer felt like insurmountable obstacles; they were merely stepping stones on my path to success.

I was reminded that the key to resilience was not just in enduring hardships but also in finding strength through support and self-belief.

Ashley continued to be my unwavering source of support, offering encouragement and helping me stay motivated.

She was also delighted to hear about the positive change in my perspective, and together we explored new job opportunities and career paths.

One evening, as the sun began to set, I decided to revisit the beach where Sebastian and I had shared our heartfelt conversation, turns out it wasn't far from home.

The tranquil beauty of the coastline and the vast expanse of the sea felt like a sanctuary, a place where I could reflect and gather my thoughts.

Sitting on the same spot where we had talked, I gazed at the horizon, thinking about my dreams and goals. The same waves that had whispered hope now seemed to echo my determination. I knew it was only a matter of time before I found the right opportunity.

Just as I was about to leave the beach, my phone rang. It was an unfamiliar number, but I answered it with curiosity. To my surprise, the voice on the other end was from the Forest Enterprise, the same company that had previously turned me down.

"Hello, this is Olivia Hunter," I said.

"Olivia, this is John King from Forest Enterprise. I hope you're doing well. I wanted to reach out to you personally."

My heart raced with anticipation. "Hello, Mr. King. I appreciate your call."

He continued, "I wanted to inform you that circumstances have changed, and we find ourselves in need of a candidate with your qualifications sooner than we anticipated. We believe you'd be an excellent fit for the role."

I could hardly believe my ears. "Are you offering me the job?"

"Yes, Olivia, we are. We'd like to extend a formal offer of employment to you. Your impressive qualifications and the way you handled the previous interview left a lasting impression, all other details will be sent with the letter".

Tears of joy welled up in my eyes. I had faced disappointment and doubt, but this moment was proof that resilience and determination could lead to success.

I accepted the job offer with gratitude, my heart brimming with hope and a deep appreciation for the support of friends like Ashley and the unexpected friendship I had found in Sebastian. As I stood on the beach where I had once felt lost, I now felt found and ready to embrace a brighter future.

The beach that had witnessed the turning point in my life now held a special place in my heart. It was a reminder that life could be full of surprises, and sometimes, they could lead to the most beautiful moments.

Wiping away the tears that were now rolling down my eyes I scrolled through my contacts and called Ashley. It was around the time that she leaves work so hopefully she answers.

The phone rang as I held it to my ear nervously, I heard a pang then I heard Ashley's voice. Not letting her finish I screamed "I got the job, Forest enterprise called me back, I got the job Ash."

"Ahhhhhhh, I'm so happy for you Liv, so happy. When did they call you, did something happen to the other person they accepted? I wouldn't know because that's not my department and the company is pretty big."

"They called just now, and I don't know what happened they just said there has been a change in events"

"Hmm, well I'm glad you got the job babe, when do you start?"

"I don't know, they said they were going to send the details but I got he job so I just had to call you first"

"Thats my girl, hey I'm gonna come over later so we came celebrate, see you later and congratulations again, you see everything is looking up for you. I told you didn't I?"

"Yeah, yeah whatever", I said laughing.

"Alright bye".

"Bye".

"Hanging up the phone I decided to go home, excited to share the news with Sebastian. I was walking home when I decided to update Sofia, she screamed in my ear just as Ashley did when I told her.

She told me she was going to come over to celebrate. I swear that girl lives and breathe alcohol. I knew that Ashley coming over to celebrate was probably her just buying pizza and few drinks.

Ashley was a bit of an introvert, she doesn't really like going out that much and she doesn't really like crowds. Don't get me wrong she will go out, she just doesn't do it often. Especially if it isn't with me but I'm slowly turning her into an extrovert.

I walked a good 25 minutes before I reached home and went straight to Sebastian's apartment. I was about to knock on the door when I noticed that it was opened.

My heart started racing out of fear, I could feel my pulse in my fingers and I could hear my heartbeat in my ear.

I slowly pushed open the door, silently praying that he's okay. I went inside dialing 911 just in case but not sending it off.

I've seen enough movies to know that this was probably not a good idea but I went anyway,maybe it was because of how excited I was.

The adrenaline was clearly still there so I felt a little confident that I could do something.

I walked in the living room and looked in the kitchen, nothing. I then decided to go into his bedroom and to say I was shocked was an understatement.

Standing there in a loose T-shirt and a pair of gray sweatpants painting what seems to be a forest was the one and only Sebastian himself.

I waited until he removed the brush from the canvas before I made my self known. "Are you serious?".

Jumping he quickly turned around "Oh shit, What the heck Liv".

"Are you trying to kill me?How did you even get in?".

I looked at him like he was crazy "you left your door opened I thought someone broke in".

Scratching his head he looked around confused then a look of realization came upon his face "Oh yeah I cracked it because I was painting and I wanted to get as much breeze in as possible".

"You have no idea how worried I was, I literally dialed 911", I said, holding up my phone for him to see.

Putting down his brush he came up to me in an attempt to hug me but I backed away "aww, you care".

"No I don't".

"You do".

"I don't"

"Whatever helps you sleep at night hun".

Rolling my eyes I looked behind him at the painting "I didn't know you painted, that looks amazing."

Looking behind him he answered "yeah, it's a little hobby I have, I started it as a way to get my feelings out you, then I found out that I actually have a passion for it. So now I do it anytime I'm free".

"Wow, you're a really talented guy".

"Thank you, I try".

"I try to learn as much as I can, life is short so why spend it doing one thing."

"True, I can't paint to save my life though but I would want to learn some day"

"I can teach you if you want"

Smiling I said "That would be awesome but be warned you're probably gonna think I'm pathetic when you see me painting for the first time"

Shaking his head he said "I would never think that".

We stared at each other in silence until I looked away and he cleared his throat.

"Are you okay though?", I asked.

"Yeah I'm okay"

"You sure?"

"Yes"

"So what's up?", he said looking back at me

"Oh I wanted to tell you that I got the job.

"No way, congratulations Liv", he said smiling.

"Yeah, they called me earlier"

"I'm proud of you"

Those words alone made me want to tear up so I walked up to him and hugged him as the tears fell. He hugged me back rubbing my back soothingly. "It's okay, you're okay"

Pulling away from him I looked up at him "Thank you really, for everything."

He looked down at me and said "You're welcome and don't ever think that you aren't good enough because you are"

Nodding I left his apartment and went back to mine. As I sat down on my bed I couldn't help but smile.

Finally!!!, she got the job

Chapter 13

The evening was awash with warm tones as the sun dipped below the horizon, casting a gentle, golden glow over the city. Ashley and Sofia had gathered in my living room, forming a circle of laughter.

The aroma of pizza filled the air, and glasses of sparkling grape juice were raised in a toast to celebrate my job offer.

Sofia, ever the lively spirit, couldn't contain her excitement. "Liv, this calls for a grand celebration! You got the job, and nothing says 'success' like pizza and sparkling grape juice."

"Atleast you didn't get alcohol Sof", I said laughing while raising my glass.

Ashley chuckled and raised her glass. "Cheers to Liv, the newest addition to the Forest Enterprise team. We always knew you were destined for great things."

We clinked our glasses together, and I couldn't help but feel grateful for friends who had stood by me through thick and thin.

Sofia, with her infectious enthusiasm, leaned forward. "So, tell us all the details. When do you start? What's the job all about?"

I grinned and took a bite of pizza before answering. "I'll get all the official details with my offer letter, but the role is a receptionist. I will be greeting and welcoming guests as soon as they arrive at the office, directing visitors to the appropriate person and office, answering and forwarding incoming phone calls, ensuring the reception area is tidy and presentable, with all necessary stationery and material etc.

Sofia, always curious, had more questions. "What about the team? Do you know your future colleagues?"

I shook my head. "Not yet, but I'm looking forward to meeting them. It'll be a new adventure."

"I'm really glad you got the job Liv,", Ashley said.

"Me too", Sofia answered.

"Soo, Who's Sebastian?", Sofia suddenly asked.

I immediately stopped chewing and looked at them "How do you know Sebastian?"

"Ashley told me he took you home the other day".

Looking at Ashley I raised my brows at her to which she just shrugged.

With a playful glint in her eye, Ashley said, "Liv, you mentioned this mysterious friend who brought you home . Tell us more about him."

Sofia leaned forward, clearly interested. "Yes, don't leave us hanging, Liv. Who is this Sebastian?"

I chuckled, realizing that they were eager to hear more about the person who had played a significant role in my recent journey. "Alright, alright, I'll spill the details. Sebastian is my neighbor, and we met quite unexpectedly on the be one day.

He's, well, a bit of a troublemaker, but he has a good heart. When I found out I didn't get the job I interviewed for, he was there to comfort me. We spent some time together, and I realized he's someone I want to be friends with."

Sofia raised an eyebrow, her curiosity piqued. "A troublemaker with a good heart? That's an interesting combination."

I nodded. "It is. He's not what he appears to be at first glance. But I value his friendship, and I feel comfortable around him."

Ashley smiled. "It sounds like he made a real impact on you, Liv."

I couldn't help but blush. "Yes, he did. He helped me through a tough time, and I'm grateful for that."

Sofia, always the romantic at heart, chimed in, "You know, Liv, it almost sounds like a movie script. Have you considered that there might be more to this friendship?"

I laughed, dismissing the idea of romance. "Come on, Sofia, it's not like that. He's just a friend, and I'm getting a new job. That's exciting enough for me."

Ashley, ever perceptive, decided to tease me. "Liv, you never know what might happen. Life has its own way of surprising us. Sometimes, friendships can turn into something more."

"Yeah, maybe you have a crush on him", Sofia chimed in.

I playfully rolled my eyes at Ashley's comment. "You're both incorrigible. Let's focus on celebrating my job offer instead."

The hours passed in the company of cherished friends, and the excitement about my new job blended with the joy of having these two incredible women by my side.

We laughed, we dreamed, and we relished the simple beauty of friendship, celebrating not only my success but the bond that had grown stronger with each passing day.

The evening was a testament to the power of resilience, support, and shared dreams, and I knew that no matter what lay ahead in my new job, I had friends who would stand with me through it all.

The conversation continued with good-natured teasing and dreams for the future. Whether it was about my new job, Ashley's novel, Sofia's travel plans, or the unexpected friendship with Sebastian, the evening was a testament to the bonds that formed through shared experiences, support, and laughter.

As the night grew darker, I couldn't help but think about what Ashley had said.

Maybe life had a way of surprising us, and perhaps my story with Sebastian was only just beginning.

CHAPTER 14

I had gotten the letter and I quickly started working, I was now able to pay my rent and buy food. I was also able to have extra money to buy other things I needed. Life was looking better for me and for the first time in a long time I was happy.

With a new job secured and the weight of disappointment lifted, I found myself with more time to focus on what truly mattered.

It also gave me the opportunity to spend more time with Sebastian, a person who had entered my life unexpectedly but had quickly become an important part of it.

Sebastian and I continued to meet up, not just in chance encounters, but with the intention of spending time together. Whether it was a quiet coffee at a local café or a leisurely stroll through the park, our conversations deepened, and our connection grew stronger.

We shared stories of our dreams, and the lessons life had taught us. I learned about his love for adventure and how he had traveled to remote places to capture the essence of untouched landscapes through his photography. He was a free spirit, and being around him made me realize that there was a world beyond the confines of my worries and disappointments.

Sebastian's presence had a calming effect on me. He listened with genuine interest when I talked about my job, my ambitions, and my insecurities. He was quick to offer encouragement and reassurance, reminding me that life was a journey with its ups and downs, and that I had the strength to face any challenge.

We discovered common interests in art, books, music, and a shared love for the outdoors. Sebastian introduced me to hiking, and we embarked on a few memorable weekend adventures. The beauty of nature and the sense of accomplishment that came with each hike brought a fresh perspective to my life.

One sunny afternoon, we decided to visit a nearby botanical garden. The lush greenery, the vibrant colors of the flowers, and the scent of blooming blossoms enveloped us as we walked through the winding paths. Sebastian's knowledge of plant life and his passion for photography combined to create a memorable experience. We shared laughter, took photos, and marveled at the wonders of the natural world.

As time passed, it became clear that our connection had deepened into a meaningful friendship. The doubts and frustrations that had once clouded my thoughts now seemed like distant memories, replaced by the warmth of hope and the support of a friend who had been there when I needed it most.

I realized that life had a way of surprising us, not just with disappointments but also with unexpected friendships and moments of connection.

With Sebastian by my side, I felt ready to face whatever challenges lay ahead, knowing that I had another friend who believed in me and a future that held the promise of endless possibilities.

Our conversations became a highlight of the time we spent together. It was during these moments that I truly got to know Sebastian, not just as a friend, but as someone with a depth of character and an intriguing perspective on life.

One evening, as we sat in a cozy corner of a local café, sipping on our respective drinks, I decided to broach a topic that had been on my mind.

"Sebastian," I began, "you've been to so many places and seen the world through your photography. What is it that draws you to those remote locations and uncharted landscapes?"

He took a thoughtful sip of his coffee before replying, "It's the untamed beauty of nature, the feeling of being in a place where human influence is minimal, if at all. These locations remind me of the raw, unfiltered aspects of our planet, and I want to capture that essence through my photographs. There's a sense of wonder and serenity in those places that's hard to find in our busy, urban lives."

I nodded, captivated by his passion for nature. "It sounds incredible. I've always been drawn to the idea of traveling and exploring, but life's demands often make it feel like a distant dream."

Sebastian's eyes sparkled as he said, "Dreams are meant to be pursued, Olivia. There's a big world out there waiting to be explored, and the experiences gained along the way can be truly transformative. Don't let your current circumstances hold you back."

His words resonated with me, and I couldn't help but ask, "Have you ever faced setbacks or challenges while pursuing your photography and adventures?"

Sebastian leaned back in his chair, a thoughtful expression on his face. "Oh, many, Olivia. I've encountered unexpected weather conditions, logistical issues, and moments when I questioned whether I was on the right path. But those challenges, as daunting as they may seem, are also part of the journey. They teach you resilience and make the triumphs even more rewarding."

It was comforting to hear that even someone as adventurous as Sebastian had faced setbacks. It made my own challenges seem less insurmountable. I continued, "What keeps you going, despite the setbacks?"

He smiled warmly. "The sheer love for what I do. The feeling of being in the right place at the right time, capturing a breathtaking sunset or the dance of the Northern Lights. It's moments like those that remind me why I embarked on this path. And, of course, the people I meet along the way, like you."

I looked down at my coffee as my cheeks started to get hot. I refused to believe that I had a crush on Sebastian, don't get me wrong he's funny, talented, charming and even an asshole at times but I just can't have a crush on him. I was finally having a bit of luck and I refused to let go of it, so ignoring the feeling I looked back at Sebastian and we continued our conversation.

"Are you okay Liv?"Seb asked, suddenly snapping me out of my thoughts.

"Yeah, yeah, I'm fine just continue talking".

He put his cup down and looked at me "Hey do you want to get out of here?"

Looking around I nodded "Yeah sure where do you want to go?".

"We can just go where the wind takes us".

I was about to get up but stopped when I heard what he said, "Sebastian be realistic", I said laughing.

Smiling, he answered "I am".

He got up and I realized he was looking for something maybe his wallet "What are you doing?, I asked.

"I'm looking for my wallet, here's the keys to the car. I'll be there in a sec."

I grabbed the keys, my coffee, my phone and my bag and went outside to where he parked his car. He parked a good 2 minutes away from the coffee shop so it didn't take long before I reached there.

I was walking to his Toyota Yaris when I spotted a few men leaning on the hood, stopping I contemplated whether I should go up to them or wait for Sebastian. I looked around and saw no sign of him so I decided to just go up to the men instead.

They were tall, muscular and looked like they could squish me like a bug, but I put on my big girl shoes and went over to them.

"Ehem", I cleared my throat causing them to look at me.

"You're on my car and I want to get going so..."

"This your car, little girl?"

"That's what I just said, are you deaf or just slow?", I asked rolling my eyes. I probably shouldn't have said that because one of the men stepped towards me and pointed his finger in my face while putting on his best I'm a bad guy face, I laughed at the joke but stopped when I realized he was starting to grab my hand forcefully, probably causing a bruise.

"Let go of me, Help!,Help!", I shouted as the guy started to drag me towards some bushes.

I tried pulling away from him but he wouldn't budge. "Help!, I tried shouting again but the man covered my mouth so my screams came out muffled. I looked around and there was no one in sight. Where the heck is everyone this is a public place for crying out loud and more importantly where is Sebastian?

God must have heard my cry because I heard someone say something causing us to freeze.

"Let her go"

The man stopped and spun us around to face the person but I already knew who it was. I knew who it was because that voice was the only voice that sent a shiver down my spine but,I'm never telling him that.

I turned around and saw that the other guy was nowhere near the scene and Sebastian now had a gun pointed to my kidnapper's head. "I said let her go", Seb said, raising his voice.

"Put the gun down -"

"Don't even think about it, let her go or else you won't live to see the light of day again", he threatened.

"Okay,okay, fine, I'll let her go", the man said, pushing me towards Sebastian.

"Get out of here"

"Bu-"

"I said get the heck out of here man"

I watched as the man hesitantly ran off leaving us alone.

Sebastian grabbed my shoulder, turned me around and scanned my body looking for injuries. When he saw none he hugged me, holding me tight.

"I thought, I, I'm so sorry Liv",

I pulled away and realized that he still had the gun in his hand. He caught me staring at it so he quickly dropped it and held out his hands towards me.

"Liv it's not what it looks like I promise."

Shaking my head I backed away even further from him "Who the hell are you?"

umm.....Remember to vote and comment!!

CHAPTER 15

"Who the hell are you?, answer me". I shouted.

"Liv if you just let me explain, let's just get out of here", he said looking around.

"No explain right here, right now why do you have a gun"

"Okay fine, I wanted to buy some flowers for you and I did but when I was coming back I saw a guy dragging you away,.I realized the one behind him had a gun so I sneaked up behind him and knocked him in the head with the vase. He was a bit far from you so you didn't hear. I hurried and caught up to you and that's when you heard me."

I looked at him in disbelief "Seb, I can't have any drama in my life right now, so if you're telling me a li-"

He quickly grabbed my face so I could look at him "I promise, I'm not lying".

I slowly nodded causing him to sigh in relief as he let me go. Grabbing my hand he pulled me towards his car and we got in. "Are you okay?", he asked.

"Yeah I'm okay, just a little bit shaken up but I'm use to it you know".

Sebastian looked away from the road and looked at me for a second "What do you mean?".

I laughed causing him to look at me worriedly "What do you want from me?"

"Sorry?"

"You're here with me and supporting me and telling me I'm beautiful, surely you must have some agenda here so what do you want?, because if you're here because you want a relationship with me, you might as well leave now".

"Liv I-"

"I'm bad news Sebastian, bad news. Just leave, you'll be doing yourself a favour", I said cutting him off.

Sebastian didn't answer so I started laughing again, I laughed so hard until I felt tears coming to my eyes. "I nearly got kidnapped", I said while continue laughing. "That's a first".

I suddenly jerked forward as the car came to a halt. "What are you doing?"

He took off his seat belt and turned towards me. "My dad left my mom and I when I was 9 years old. He left her with no money and my mom had to juggle two jobs just so we could have food on the table. My mom could have given up when times got hard and trust me, times did get hard but she loved me and we managed, barely but we managed.

My mom died when I was 18 and I, I will forever be grateful for her", he said, closing his eyes for a second before reopening them to continue.

"We don't talk alot about our past life. As a matter of fact we don't talk about it at all but when I saw you that day, I saw a person who needed a friend more than anything. I know I mess around a lot but I'm a pretty serious guy.

So look at me good and listen well, I'm not leaving, I don't have any hidden agendas. I'm here because I want to be here for you and I won't give up on you just because you feel like it. I wasn't raised to give up and I don't plan on starting now".

We were now breathing heavily as I stared at him and him at me. I opened my mouth to answer but stopped when a car started honking at us, followed by other vehicles. I looked around and that's when I realized we were in the road.

"Sebastian, go, go, we're holding up traffic".

"Not until you understand".

I looked behind me at the people now pushing their heads through their cars cursing. "Okay yes I understand, now drive please".

Nodding he quickly put back on his seatbelt and we drove off.

"You're crazy you know that right?".

"Only crazy for you", he said winking causing butterflies to form in my stomach.

I hissed my teeth as I looked out the window so he wouldn't see me blushing.

5 minutes passed and I still didn't know where we were going. "Are you taking me somewhere to kidnap me?".

"Yes".

"Come on Sebastian",

"I'm coming soon, how about you?"

Confused I looked at him "huh?"

He glanced at me smirking then looked back at the road.

My eyes widened in shock when I realized what he meant. I slapped his shoulder in annoyance "you are just ugh", I said in frustration.

"Hey!, no hitting the driver".

"I swear you have two different personalites sometimes".

"Why do you say that?".

"Sometimes you're cocky and then sometimes you're nice and gentle"

Laughing he said "That's just me for you".

I smiled as I realized he came to a stop. I looked around and realized we were at a park.

Getting out of the car I looked at him and saw that he was getting something from the car that I later realized was a camera.

"Are you going to show me how to take pictures?"

"I can but that's not why we're here", he said walking up to me.

"Why then".

"I always tell you that you're beautiful because I mean it, now it's time for you to see it too".

"You're going to take my picture?"

"Yes", he answered smiling.

"Okay, come on", he said guiding me towards a bench where I sat and he snapped a few pictures of me.

We then went on to a pond where I sat and played with a duck. "Hi, little guy or girl, hey is he a guy or girl", I asked.

"I have no idea, look under his ass".

Laughing I said "I don't think that's how you know"

"Oh well"

We snapped a few more there then we moved to some trees where he snapped a few more.

Just then I got an idea, I took out my phone and took a picture of him taking a picture of me.

"Come here", I called him and he came over. So I put the phone on selfie and started taking pictures of the both of us.

I stuck out my tongue and he did the same causing me to giggle. I scrolled through the pictures and smiled sending them to him. "Okay my turn, give me the camera".

Hesitantly he passed it to me and forced a smile. "Gosh you don't have to look so scared, I'm not going to drop it"

"Haha, I wasn't worried"

I glared at him and made him show me how to use it. I took a few of him and few of the ducks.

The sun was going down so we decided to head back home. We reached my door and before I went in I turned around and looked at him. "I had a nice time today Seb thank you".

"You're welcome Liv".

I went up to him and gave him a kiss on his cheek "bye".

"Bye", he said as I went inside.

I know you might be like okay, what was the purpose of that but everything will come to light soon. Bye

CHAPTER 16

The blast of my alarm woke me up letting me know I'm alive to see a next next day. I rolled over groaning to turn off the alarm and sat up on the bed staring out of space for a good five minutes.

After I finished I peeked through the window and smiled. I then got up, stretched and went to the bathroom to start my morning routine. It was now 5 am and I had to get to work buy 8.

I did my business, brushed my teeth and did my hair. I currently had in braids so all I did was my edges and added some mousse to my hair to refresh it. I then wrapped my hair so it would stay.

I checked the time and saw that it was just 5:15 am. Time to get some food I thought.

I went to the kitchen and started making something to eat so I put the pot on fire and as I waited for it to heat up I grabbed my phone and decided to put on some music.

"Smooth like butter, like a criminal under cover, hot like summer, yeah you making me sweat like that"

I grabbed a spoon using it as my mircophone and continued singing. I made breakfast as I sang and danced around the kitchen. Not having a care in the world.

I was happy, my life was good, I had a good job, good friends and a guy. I suddenly started blushing as I thought about Sebastian.

We have been close for a while now. I wonder if I should ask him to be with me. That would be probably be weird. Crap!, what if he doesn't even like me that way and all the flirting was just him missing around?.

I sat down about to eat as I tried to shake away the negative thoughts. I made an omlete and some ginger tea, I really love tea, with bread and I was about to take a bite when a ping alerted me that I had received a notification.

Good morning Liv, hope you have a good day today see you later❤

~Sebastian.

Okay there's no way I'm that delustional, he clearly has something for me. I'm going to ask him to be my boyfriend. Woah that sounded weird I thought as I smiled.

I bit down on my lip trying to decide what to text back but just decided to send

"Good morning, thanks and hope you have a good day too"❤~Liv

He must be off to work right now. Gosh I hope he doesn't reject me because I cannot afford to get rejected today. I finished my breakfast then went to have a shower and did some light makeup. I quickly got dressed and head out the door.

I went to the bus stop trying to get a taxi because well I can't afford a car as yet but I'm saving to get to one so I don't have to wait on a bus or taxi everyday.

I stood for a good 15 minutes before I finally got drive. I checked the time as I reached at work. Right on time I thought.

I went to the entrance and showed my I.D before entering the premises. It still amazes me how huge this place is.

It was five floors tall, with intricate designs on the outside and in. The modern architectural marvel stands proudly at the heart of the city. Its exterior is a symphony of steel, concrete, and glass.

The front of the building, spanning from the ground to the fifth floor, is entirely constructed of sleek, transparent glass panels, which reflect the cityscape during the day and emit a warm, inviting glow at night that shone beautifully.

Maybe one day I'll start a business of my own. I've always wanted to start one but my life has been one crap after the other.

I went in the elevator and pressed the floor I worked on. It was the fifth floor where the ceo worked. I am the person you see before you see him.

As I was standing in the elevator I started humming that one bts song. I have no idea why it's been stuck in my head since yesterday.

The elevator stopped and I went into the office. I was at the reception area in front of the ceo.

I checked in and got started on working immediately. The ceo was not in yet but I had some paper work to be done and some emails to answer.

30 minutes passed when I heard a ding causing me to look up. The elevator opened and I saw the ceo and his personal assistant walking closely behind him.

I cleared my throat as I waited for him to pass by so I could greet him. "Good morning Mr. Blackhood, how are you doing today?".

He stopped and turned to me "Not too bad Olivia, Good morning. Do you have the documents ready that I asked for yesterday?".

I couldn't help but stare at him, Jonathan Anderson, the CEO of a multinational corporation, a striking figure, standing at 6'3" with a commanding presence.

His rugged, chiseled features and strong jawline give him an air of confidence and authority. He has a deep, resonant voice that commands attention in any room.

Jonathan's salt-and-pepper hair is meticulously groomed, adding a touch of maturity to his appearance. His piercing steel-blue eyes seem to miss nothing and convey his sharp intellect. He's often seen in well-tailored suits that accentuate his tall and athletic build, exuding both professionalism and style.

Despite his imposing presence, Jonathan's warm smile and charismatic demeanor put people at ease. He has a firm handshake, which is often the first impression that he leaves on those he meets. His attire is typically completed with designer shoes and a classic wristwatch, symbolizing his attention to detail and appreciation for the finer things in life.

Overall, Jonathan Anderson is a CEO who combines a strong, authoritative appearance with a personable and approachable demeanor, making him a charismatic leader who knows how to make a lasting impression, and it was why I respected him so much.

He's not like those typical CEO assholes. He was actually nice. Snapping out of my thoughts I quickly answered him.

"Yes sir, here they are", I said handing them the documents.

"hmm, I have a meeting today right?"

"yes sir, at one pm".

"Reschedule it, I have a personal issue I need to handle"

"Okay sir, noted"

He then walked off and I immediately got started on working.

○●○●○●○●○●○●○

I glanced at the clock now realizing that it 12, time for lunch I thought as I left my desk and headed to the lunch room. I went in and scanned the area looking for a familiar set of hazel eyes. Finding them I quickly went over and took a seat beside her "Hey Ash".

She immediately turned around and smiled. "Hey Liv".

"What's up?"

"Nothing just here having lunch"

Nodding, I told her I was going to buy something. I got up and bought my food and a drink.

While standing in the line I heard my coworkers whispering. "Did you hear about the-", I didn't hear anything more because they either stopped or lowered their voice.

Shaking my head as I collected my food and left. Why do people like gossiping so much?

I sat back down at the table with Ashley where she was sitting with a few other coworkers.

"Olivia right?", a fair looking woman asked.

"Yeah that's me "

"How are you?"

I looked at Ashley but she only shrugged. I looked back at the lady and smiled. "I'm great, the company is quite nice, I'm enjoying my time here".

Nodding she asked again leaning closer to me "you must be enjoying your time here if you get access to seeing Johnathan for so long."

Ashley suddenly choked on her apple and laughed.

I didn't look at her as I answered the woman. "He's like 50", I said raising my brows.

"The older the better hun", she said winking at me. "I bet his dic-"

"Okayyy Sash, we're done here", Asley said laughing. "Come on Liv, I'm gonna use the bathroom.

Agreeing I got up and quickly swallowed the last piece of chicken. We walked to the bathroom and went inside. "Sorry about her, she can be a lot", Ash said smiling.

"I'm surprised your friends with her though, you're kinda shy", I said to which she only shrugged. "We're more like work friends."

Entering the stall, I went in and did my business when I heard a voice "I cannot believe that Johnathan is involved in that, I know he looks serious but that is another thing.

"I know, money laundering is a big deal right,what if he finds out we know?

You'll keep your mouth shut if you know what's best for you. I didn't risk my ass to look at those files for you to be chatting so much.

Okay, I won't say anything I promise. But what are you going to do with the information?

You don't need to know that just keep your mouth shut and I'll tell you when I need you. "

It was quiet for a minute then I heard them exciting the bathroom. I waited a minute before I came out of the stall and looked around. "Ashley!", I whisper shouted.

"Yes", she answered coming out as well.

"Did you just hear that?", I asked

"Yes but forget anything you just heard Liv, he can be dangerous"

"But-"

"But nothing, just forget it, come on lunch is up we have work to do".

Not answering her we washed our hands and excited the bathroom. We went our separate ways since she worked in a different department.

I went back to my desk and started working but I found myself constantly glancing at Mr Blackhood's office.

There was something calling me to investigate, I had to see what was going on, I had to.

Vote and comment if you like.

CHAPTER 17

I t was now 1pm and Mr. Blackhood was about to leave the office for a personal matter. I hovered near his office, feigning focus on a stack of papers while my eyes were fixated on the corridor.

The distant hum of office activity masked the drumming of my anxious heart. A subdued conversation reached me as I saw him coming out with his personal assistant trailing behind him five minutes later.

Mr. Blackhood emerged, his face etched with solemnity.

"Mr.blackhood is everything okay?" I asked, injecting a carefully measured concern into my voice.

He sighed, weariness evident. "Liv, I'm leaving now and I might be gone for a few hours. Can you hold down the fort while I'm away?"

With a reassuring smile, I nodded. "Of course, Mr. Thompson. Don't worry about anything. We've got it covered here."

"Thank you, Liv. I appreciate it." His gaze lingered briefly, gratitude and fatigue mingling. Guilt tugged at me, knowing I was about to exploit his absence. But I was too determined to let that get to me so I pushed away the feeling.

As Mr. Blackhood and his assistant walked away, I maintained my facade until he disappeared around a corner. The unguarded office door beckoned, its mysteries calling out to me.

A deep breath steadied my nerves; the clandestine dance had begun, and I was poised to navigate the delicate balance between loyalty and curiosity.

My heart raced as I approached my boss's office, the hallway stretching like a corridor of anxiety. The door loomed ahead, and with each step, the weight of my clandestine mission pressed on my shoulders.

I took a deep breath, my trembling hand reaching for the doorknob. The subtle creak of the door made me wince, and I glanced around, paranoia tightening my nerves.

Ashley's words echoing in my head but I pushed them out. There was this feeling that I had, all I know is that I needed to know what he's hiding. But, there's also the possibility of me dying but what the heck I doubt my life can get worse than this.

Once inside I held my breath and hesitated, torn between curiosity and fear.

My eyes scanned the room, searching for any sign of the coveted information. Drawers lined the mahogany desk like silent sentinels, tempting me with the unknown. I tiptoed towards them, my steps betraying the rhythm of my racing heart. As I pulled open the first drawer, a surge of adrenaline coursed through my veins.

Fingers fumbled through files, careful not to make a sound. The papers rustled under my touch, echoing in the silence of the room. My eyes darted nervously towards the closed door, every distant murmur amplifying in my ears.

A soft beep startled me. I froze, panic gripping me. I glanced at the computer screen on my boss's desk – a screensaver teasing me with its idle dance. The urge to check for emails, to delve into the digital labyrinth of information, wrestled with me caution.

I approached the computer, hesitating before gingerly tapping the mouse. The screen flickered to life, revealing a password prompt. My mind raced as I tried to recall any clues that might unlock the gateway to secrets. I bit my lip, anxiety intensifying with each failed attempt.

Time seemed to stretch, and the office walls seemed like they were closing in. The air grew heavier with the weight of my actions. My palms were clammy, and my heart threatened to betray me with its erratic beat. I forced myself to focus, combing through the desk and computer for any shred of information.

Just as desperation started to claw at my resolve, my eyes caught a folder tucked away in a corner. Its label hinted at confidentiality, and hope rekindled in my chest. With trembling hands, I opened it, revealing a group of documents that could unlock the mysteries I sought.

My hands trembled as I carefully pulled out the hidden folder, its label whispering promises of revelation. The weight of anticipation hung in the air as I opened it, scanning through the documents that laid bare the secrets Mr. Blackhood harbored.

Shock seized me as I discovered the illegal activities woven into the fabric of his dealings. The implications unfurled like a sinister tapestry, leaving me breathless and uneasy. But it was the unexpected connection that sent a chill down my spine – my parents' names embedded in the midst of it all.

A wave of conflicting emotions crashed over me. Disbelief mingled with a sense of betrayal, and the air in the room grew heavy with the weight of revelation. My mind raced, grappling with the realization that my parents, the ones that I grew up watching all these years , were entangled in this illicit web.

The images of my family clashed with the harsh reality laid out before me. Questions swirled in my mind, and the shock slowly gave way to a bitter mix of confusion and hurt.

How could they keep this from me? Was this why they hated me?

As the truth sank in, I found myself questioning everything –what the heck was going on? The room seemed to close in around me, and I was left grappling with the tangled mess of emotions and revelations that now defined my understanding of family.

As I skipped through the file I saw multiple financial transactions, offshore accounts, and coded communications, suggesting the company is deeply involved in money laundering.

Detailed records expose a network of connections to high-profile figures, raising questions about the extent of corruption and the potential impact on the economy.

But the only question I have is why my parents are involved. I try searching around for more information but I don't find any. I pulled at my hair in frustration.

I was about to place everything back in it's place when I heard a voice.

"What do you think you're doing?"

You remember when I said it couldn't get much worse than this?, it just did.

Oh oh, what do you guys think?, let me know your predictions in the comments..

CHAPTER 18

I slowly turned around and was shocked to see Cecile, Mr. Blackhood's personal assistant. "I-I", I said, trying to gather my thoughts.

Say something Olivia

The room felt stifling as she awaited a response, a heavy silence hanging in the air, beads of sweat started forming my forehead, I finally managed to stammer out an excuse about a misplaced file. Cecile, unimpressed, raises an eyebrow, scrutinizing the shaky explanation.

In a measured tone, she says, "Misplaced files don't usually end up in the hands of employees who have no business with them. Explain yourself, now."

Palms clammy I fumble through a half-hearted explanation, attempting to divert suspicion. However, she's seasoned in reading people and sees through the flimsy story. The tension escalates as her gaze intensifies, demanding the truth.

"You've stumbled onto something you shouldn't have," she asserts, a hint of warning in her voice.

"This company has secrets, but they're not for your eyes. What were you hoping to find?"

"I-um", I stammered.

Grabbing the files from me she said "I won't say anything but if you mention any of this to anyone, you will not like what happens", she threatened.

I gulped and ran out of the room. I went to the bathroom and released a breath I didn't realize I was holding.

I placed a hand over my heart as I tried to calm it down. What just happened? I nearly died back there. If Johnathan had caught me-, I just knew I wouldn't make it out alive.

I just hope Cecile doesn't tell on me. I don't know what I would do if that were to happen.

Taking out my phone I went to Ashley's name hovering over the call button, I contemplated whether I should call her or not.

She did warn me not to do anything but the question is why?, does she know about the shady business?. Who else knows?Does she know about my parents?.

Too many questions were flooding my head as I decided not to tell her. I just could not trust anyone right now. I splashed some water on my face and dried it as I went back to my desk.

I wanted to leave but I couldn't especially since Johnathan wasn't here. I looked at the time and saw that it was 1:30pm. Sighing I just went back to work. I would just have to forget everything that happened for now.

It was 4pm when Mr. Blackhood stormed into his office and slammed the door. I looked at it nervously, did he find out?.

I stared at the door but jumped when I heard him call me into his office. Pausing I looked around, okay this is it. I'm dead aren't I?.

I'm too young, I haven't lived yet, what do I do?. I swallowed and decided to just face his wrath as I nervously opened his door. "You called sir?", I said, my voice shaking.

"Yes, you can go home now", he said without looking up. "Umm, are you firing me?"

Looking up he raised a brow at me "Why would I fire you?".

"Oh,oh, no reason, thank you sir, enjoy the rest of your evening", I said, my eyes glancing at Cecile who was seated in the corner of the room before walking out.

I quickly gathered my things and got out of the building and quickly went home.

○●○●○●○●○●○●○●○●○●○●○●○●○●○●○

I quickly went inside, took off my clothes and had a shower. I can't believe what happened today. My boss, my parents.

I felt like I know so little about my parents but then again I don't know anything about them. But, I didn't think they would be capable of that. But then again parents that treat their kid like that definitely have potential to do anything.

The only question that keeps racking my brain is why. I stepped out of the shower and dried myself and got in some clothes before heading to the kitchen to heat up some leftovers.

As I stood there staring out of space, my phone started ringing. Looking at it I saw that it was Sebastian. Smiling, I answered the call. "I'm picking you up at 6 tonight, dress comfortably."

"What about Hi, hello, how are you?", I said laughing.

A chorus of laughter was heard through the phone " Hi Olivia, hello Olivia, How are you Olivia?"

"See you at 6 Seb", I answered laughing.

"Bye"

Removing the phone from my ear I looked at the time and saw that it was now 5pm. Luckily I bathed already so all I had to do was fix my hair and put on some clothes.

I got ready just in time when I heard a knock on the door. Spraying some perfume on and grabbing my bag I went to open the door.

I was greeted with a smile on Sebastian's face and a bouquet of flowers in his hand. "Flowers for the lady", he said, smiling cheekily.

"When did you become so cheesy?"

"How is this chessy?"

"Anyways where are we going?", I said, rolling my eyes.

"You should roll those eyes of yours until it falls out"

I turned around and glared at him but he only smiled and grabbed my hands pulling me towards his car. We got in, I turned on the radio and the car was filled with the tunes of chase atlantic's song into it.

"Yeah I'm into it, I'm into it, says she wanna ..me later girl I'm into it."

Looking at him, I saw him glancing at me "What?"

He shrugged "nothing".

I shaked my head and continued singing while we drove along the road. 10 minutes passed and Sebastian suddenly stopped. Looking around I saw that we were at a restaurant.

"LOVERS LANE", it read.

I turned towards Seb but realized he came out and was coming out to open my door. He did and held out his hand towards me so I grabbed it and he helped me out of the car.

He held my hand as we walked up to the restaurant in silence, causing my mind to drift back to what happened today. Should I tell him?Can I trust him?.

I looked up at him and he seemed to have this determined look on his face. "Are you okay", he suddenly asked.

That's when I realized that we stopped and he was now staring at me " Yes I'm okay, just a bit lost in thought. "

"Umm, is the location nice?, I didn't know if you'd like it or not", smiling at his nervousness I nodded "It's lovely Seb, let's go inside"

We went inside and was shown our table when I realized something odd about the place. Everyone was missing, aside from the staff that is. I looked around then looked at Sebastian who was.looking at me nervously.

"What's going on?, where is everyone?"

"I rented it out for the evening"

"How can you afford to do this?"

"Umm, I've been saving for this for a while now."

Shaking my head still not understanding " Okay but why are you going through all this trouble to do this?"

"It wasn't any trouble at all Liv"

"Okay but why are you doing this?"

Rubbing his hand over his face in frustration he began speaking "I wasn't planning on doing this yet, I wanted us to eat, talk, have a good time then I would pop the question."

My heart started racing "po-pop the question?"

"As much as I want to, not that question".

I looked around and the staff was smiling. They all stood proudly as if waiting for something to happen. A violinist was playing a beautiful tune that blended gracefully with the mini waterfall in the middle of the restaurant.

"Sebastian", I called, turning around to look at him but paused when I saw him on one knee.

I widened my eyes in shock, not believing what was happening. Please don't let him propose, I can't handle this right now, my heart is beating out of my chest, my palms are sweaty. It feels like it's hotter than usual and I feel like I might faint.

Taking some deep breaths I look back down at Sebastian as he holds my hand.

Seeing him kneeling before me made my heart quickened its pace. His eyes held a mix of nervousness and sincerity. The world seemed to fade away, leaving just the two of us in that vulnerable moment.

"I've been thinking a lot about us," he began, his voice a gentle hum. "And I can't imagine my days without you in them. Will you be my girlfriend?"

My mind raced with a whirlwind of emotions, but one thing was clear – the warmth in his gaze mirrored the flutter in my chest. The weight of his question hung in the air, and as I looked into his eyes, I felt a smile tug at the corners of my lips.

"Yes," I whispered, the word carrying the weight of anticipation and joy. And just like that, our journey together took a new, sweet turn.

CHAPTER 19

An hour passed and we were currently still on our date. Laughing and creating memories that I'm sure we would remember in the future. We talked about our time together as friends and how it ended up to this moment.

"I knew I wanted to be in your life the moment I saw you to be honest, whether as a friend or boyfriend. I was willing to just be there for you."

Looking at him I smiled "You're amazing Sebastian"

Smirking he said "of course I am"

I shook my head glaring at him "way to ruin the moment"

"I'm sorry sweatheart".

Shaking my head I smiled and continue eating. The activities of today totally forgotten.

We spent another hour conversing until we decided to wrap it up for the night. We headed back to his car and he drove us home. He then parked the car infront of the building and we went upstairs and stopped Infront of my door.

He turned to me and smiled. "I had a lot of fun today girlfriend", he said winking.

"And I had a lot of fun boyfriend", I replied winking back causing him to throw his head back laughing.

He stepped closer to me causing me to back up against the door. He licked his lips as he looked down at mine then back at my eyes, causing me to mimick his actions.

I started breathing heavily as he leaned in close to my lips but not touching it as if he's giving me space incase I back out, but I leaned in causing our lips to touch.

Sebastian saw this as a sign to continue as he pulled me in closer and deepened the kiss. I wrapped my hands around his neck and he grabbed my waist pulling me even closer to him.

I felt his abs on my chest and the bulge in his pants was pressing against my stomach. I moaned as he left from my lips to my neck sucking until he was satisfied, he then went back to my lips.

I ran my fingers through his hair and occationally pulled causing him to moan. He moved his hand from my waist to my neck grabbing it forcefully but not enough to hurt me and the other he used to hold the back of my head.

Butterflies erupted in my stomach as I moaned causing him to smile against my lips. I ran my hands across his chest and was about to tell him we should take it inside when I heard my phone ringing.

Groaning Sebastian pulled away from my lips and I was left panting with my cheeks flushed. I licked my lips as he stared at me hungrily. Looking around I felt for my pocket that had the now ringing phone.

I quickly took it out hissing my teeth in annoyance, I swear if Ashley is calling me right now I am going to kill her but I hesitated when I saw that it was a number I didn't recognize.

I looked up at Seb and saw that he was still staring at me, without thinking i just answered the call and put it to my ear still maintaining eye contact with Sebastian.

A second passed and the person didn't say anything so I said hello. I heard shuffling but no response I took the phone from my ear and looked at the number again before putting the phone back at my ear. "Hello", I called again but no answer was given.

I was about to hang up when I heard someone speaking. "Listen to me well Olivia, I need you to meet me at hopelyn street in the orange building tomorrow at noon. Just go in and tell them you're there to see Mr. Smith I will be expecting you. Don't bring anybody or tell anyone we spoke. You can't trust anyone right now. I know you might be thinking then why should I trust you?, but I know you Olivia, you might not remember me but I'm your family's lawyer and I just have your best interest at heart. So just meet with me and I will give you the answers you're looking for. Remember don't tell anyone"

I didn't even get to reply before he hang up. I took the phone from my ear and looked at Sebastian who was now looking at me curiously. "Is everything okay?"

I merely nodded "Yeah everything's fine umm I'm going to get some sleep now. Thank you for the evening I will call you tomorrow", I said kissing him on the lips before heading inside.

Once I'm inside and I heard his footsteps disappear I look at my phone replaying what the man said in my head. My family's lawyer?, why do I feel like every is going so right but so wrong?, should I go?, what if its a trick?, but first my boss and now this, surely it can't be a coincidence.

But how do I know he's telling the truth?, I don't remember us having a lawyer but looking back at it now my parents were very secretive. I just thought that they didnt want to be around me.

Sighing I contemplated what I should I do. I could ignore him and potentially never find out any information as to what's going because it seems my family has a secret or I could go and find out what the heck is going on.

I sat for an hour thinking about what i should do before I made up my mind. It was final I was going to the meet up. Am I taking a huge risk trying to find out about people that don't even like me? Yes but I have to know why they don't like me. There has to be a reason.

So I went to sleep that night determined to get to the bottom of the issue.

I got up the next morning and made breakfast but not before calling in a sick leave. Cecile is probably going to be suspicious so this better me worth it.

It didn't take long for 11oclock to roll in and I left the house. I quickly texted Sebastian telling him good morning and telling him I'm at work.

I didnt want to lie but I didn't have a choice. I made sure I packed a knife in a small bag I brought with me just in case and hit the road.

At exactly 12pm I was standing outside the building I was instructed to be at. Smith's enterprise a sign on the building read. I thought it was going to be a sketchy place but it wasn't.

I stood for one more minute so I could give myself time to back out but I didn't. Instead I went inside and saw a lady at the front office. "Hi how can I help you?".

"I'm here to see Mr. Smith"

"Right this way please", she said walking infront of me leading me to a door down a corridor that read "Mr. Smith".

She turned around once we reached and smiled at me "just go right in and if you need anything else tell me know", she then walked off.

I turned towards the door clutching my bag tightly before raising my hand to knock on the door. Shortly after I heard a voice telling me to come in.

I slowly pushed open the door and went inside to see a middle aged white guy sitting at a desk. "Ugh, Mr Smith its Olivia, you called yesterday?".

Nodding he smiled "Yes I did call and I know it's you Olivia, I couldn't forget that face of yours. "

I looked at him confused which only caused him to chuckle. "Have a seat Olivia we have a lot to talk about."

A/NSo I have my ideas of what's going to happen but I want to hear your ideas. Tell me your predictions and maybe I'll change it to your idea.

Thanks again for reading

CHAPTER 20

"Well, tell me why I came here", I said eagerly. I was currently sitting in a chair across from Mr. Smith, my legs were shaking and my palms were sweating but I kept my face calm.

I was nervous, I'm not sure if I wanted to know in the first place but then again I kind of want to know, I deserve to know. But the look on his face was not helping at all. His brows were pushed up worryingly and it was not helping my anxiety. Not to mention his eyes constantly glancing at the clock behind me.

The clearing of a throat brought me out of my thoughts and I met his eyes. "There's no easy way to tell you this so I'll do my best, let's start from the beginning shall we?"

Nodding, I urged him to continue "I'm your family's lawyer. You see your family is involved in a lot of", he paused before continuing. "illegal businesses and I would cover for them to ensure they didn't get caught. I covered their tracks when it came to the law and I was very good at it.

Since you moved out I've been secretly keeping an eye on you. I know you have a job at Forest Enterprise and I know you found those documents about your parents and your boss.

"Cecile", I said shocked. Nodding he said "yes Cecile filled me in she's one of my eyes I have at the cooperation"

"That's why she didn't tell on me"

"Yes that's right"

"Please continue"

"Ahh yes as I was saying, Your family is into a lot of illegal stuff but the reason I'm telling you this is because of something that has to do with you.

"me, what do I have to do with this?"

"Your grandparents were powerful people, they had the entire country wrapped around their fingers".

My brows shot up in surprise "I knew they died but I didn't know anything about them, Why didn't I hear about them?"

"That was for a reason, your parents tried to conceal the truth from you for as long as possible"

I shook my head still not understanding "What truth?, What are you talking about?".

"Your grandparents were filthy rich Olivia and they left everything to you"

I was left gaping at the words I just heard. "Did you just say they left everything to me?, for how long now?"

Me. Smith sighed as he leaned back into his chair "the inheritance belonged to you before you were even born, it was yours all along".

I shook my head refusing to believe this "That's not possible, it I had an inheritance why wasn't I informed?"

He didn't answer but he didn't have to because it all started to come together in my head. "My parents, they hid it from me but why?, what, why would they do that unless they-", I stopped talking as my eyes widened at Mr. Smith.

"They wanted it to themselves, didn't they ?"

He merely nodded as he ran his hand over his face "Yes Olivia", Mr. Smith confirmed. "Your grandmother's wealth was substantial, and your parents, entangled in their own ambitions and financial struggles, saw it as a solution to their problems. They believed that by pushing you away, they could eliminate any potential obstacle to their claim on the inheritance."

I felt a mix of shock and betrayal, struggling to reconcile the image I had of my parents with this new, unsettling truth. "So, they used me as a pawn in their scheme?"

Mr. Smith nodded gravely. "I'm afraid so, They wanted to distance you from the inheritance. They hoped that by isolating you emotionally and manipulating the circumstances, they could ensure that you wouldn't stand in their way and the fact that they didn't exactly like you helped to make that situation easier."

"Okay but financial struggles? I thought my grandparents were rich, why would they be struggling financially and why did I get everything?, what about my parents?"

"That's how your boss comes in, he and your parents used to work together until he tricked your parents leaving them bankrupt. That company Forest enterprise was a business your grandfather started, it was passed down to your parents but they used it for money laundering.

They were bankrupt and they went to your grandparents for help, by that time she found out she was pregnant with you so she used the pregnancy card but it didn't work out as she imagined, it backfired on her. Because instead of her getting the riches of her parents, it went down to you.

Your grandparents helped them get back on their feet but that was as much help they got and one of the only reasons they helped was because of you. Your mother even tried having an abortion when she found out. But, her mother threatened to bring her in for all the illegal stuff they were involved in. Ever since they have been trying to find a way to break the inheritance but it's solid.

I felt a mix of emotions - disbelief, anger, confusion. "So that explains why they hate me."

I started laughing, really laughing. I laughed so hard my stomach started to hurt and I had to hold it. Tears welled in my eyes but I aggressively wiped them away.

"You mean to tell me all this struggle I've been through, all the shit I've been through was over as stupid inheritance", I raised my voice.

"No, there has to be another reason, tell me that's not the reason. Please tell me you're joking, this has to be a prank, where are the cameras?"I said looking around, my voice cracking.

"This is the truth Olivia, I'm sorry"

I stood up quickly causing him to do the same. "you can tell them that they can have it, I'm done with all of this, I'm done"

He only looked at me sadly and it was then that I realized the complexity of my family's secrets. Inheritance, danger, and a past I knew nothing about - it was a lot to take in. Mr. Smith looked at me with sincerity, "Olivia, you need to be vigilant. There are people who would stop at nothing to get their hands on what rightfully belongs to you.

Listen, your parents are clearly shitty people but you have a decision to make. You can let them win by giving up or you can show them that you're stronger than they think. It's up to you", he said, handing me a bunch of papers.

"When you're ready just sign this, the rest of the information is on here so you can contact me and we can go from there. This inheritance is yours Olivia it's your birthright.

I looked down at the paper and took it then looked back up at him "So what about you?"

"What about me?"

"You expect me to believe you don't get something out of this, you worked for my parents for years, how do I know this isn't their doing?"

"Fair point, but I was tired of seeing you suffer, I owe you this, I helped your parents bury the inheritance so you wouldn't find out. Trust me I know the risks of telling you this because your parents are dangerous but I'm done with them. I've downloaded some information on a drive, you need to give it to this person if anything happens. ", he says, handing me a drive and a card.

I put it along with the paper in my bag. "I know this is a lot to take in now but read through it, the sooner you sign the better so you can finally take what's yours. Here is a burner phone, text me if you have any questions, don't call just text, got it? I can't let them know that you know because of me okay?"

Nodding, I took it and pushed it in my bag. "I got it"

"Okay now go"

I was turning to leave when he called to me "And Olivia, remember that it's your birthright."

I din't answer as I opened the door and went outside. Holding my bag for dear life as I hailed a taxi and went home.

I sat down and thought about what I learned today. With a heavy heart, I absorbed the truth about my parents and the complicated web of their actions. The path ahead was unclear, but one thing was certain - I had to navigate the intricacies of this hidden legacy, even if it meant facing the people who, in their not so love, chose to keep me at arm's length.

www.ingramcontent.com/pod-product-compliance
Lightning Source LLC
Chambersburg PA
CBHW072018210726

48294CB00012B/1074